THE GOLD TRAIL

Novel by: MS /Khoeses

Self-Published
© Martha Sibila /Khoeses, 2020

Address
P O Box 4091
Windhoek
Namibia
Telephone: +264 81 605 7921
Email: khoeses@gmail.com

Edited by: Frieda Mukufa
Jeffrou's Language Consultancy
Email: jefflangconsultancy@gmail.com

Graphics Design: Shikulo Pinehas "Zulu boy"
Zuluboy AmaDaz Floor
Email: zuluboyamadazfloor@gmail.com

ISBN: 978-99945-88-63-3

Distribution by Amazon:
www.amazon.com

Dedicated to all Africans, by an African, for Africa

ACKNOWLEDGEMENTS

Dr Hylton Villet, your vote of confidence in my world enables me to dream bigger, and allow creativity to challenge me beyond the obvious limitations. You read the raw draft and respond; "It make me think back and recognize my true identity, the Nama blood that flows through my veins", I knew then that my work would resonate with many and be accepted because it speaks to the heart which wanted to embrace its native identity. Thank you for silently holding my hand.

Tia A /Khoëses, when you said that this will definitely be the one book you are looking forward to read, it affirmed and justify the project vision. I wanted to contribute to the vast African narratives to preserve our history as a people in the best possible way. I hope you will share our stories with my grandchildren to ensure that our culture and history lives on. Thank you for being an inquisitive and curious child, that made me sit up and revisit our forgotten tales for a better representation.

Tanaka Gabriel Machakaire, thank you for sitting down with me and listening to the idea from inception. I smile when I recall your words, "I wouldn't want to miss an opportunity to be part of such great creativity. Regardless of its great controversies with my belief".

To my editor and graphics designer, thank you for the willingness to work with me on this special project and asking me daring questions which send me back each time to find answers.

To all those that came before me, academics and writers both of African and Western descent, who employ their time to do extensive research and write down various African episodes of pre and post-colonial experiences, thank you. Raised in a modern society, I too stood loss and clueless of our cultural and historic past until I started reading your work and decide to search deeper for answers which could explain my identity much clearer. Indeed we ride on the backs of those that came before us.

Special thanks to my community of readers, it remains a *'dream come true'* for a writer to see his/her work in the hands of a reader. Each time you stand by me, awaiting the next instalment, I am encouraged because it affirms that the creative gift from the gods is serving its purpose.

Celebrating

Nthabeleng Madots Ramoeli, our Tiny Dots, I would have failed if I don't mention you. When you stepped into my office for the first time with your tiny feet I met a real time light worker. With your witty smile, you captivate my mind and set it on a journey beyond this world I knew. You open up a brand new, yet old world to me. A world of wonder, of magical Godly splendor, a world so divine which no man could fathom, let alone pen down. I was lost in that world, yet it was that world that show me the truth in me. That world let me to know, understand and appreciate me and the godly identity which was divinely fashioned within me. I started dreaming of that wonder, started living in the true purpose which we all are called to serve. I started being me, true and African. Surely as I ride on the shoulders of those that came before me, I'm glad the Angels orchestrated a meeting between us, not so that we celebrate in silence but blow trumpets out of proportion while sharing light to the world. Thank you for revealing yourself to me, I am because you are. As your wings expand into your divine calling, I can simple watch with gratitude and thank God for endorsing your life, I celebrate you today, yesterday and always. Thank you for lighting the path as mandated.

"I stand on the backs of those who came before me." (Vanzant, 1993)

THE GOLD TRAIL

PRELUDE

Planet C-53 has gone through tremendous changes over the centuries. There was a time, well noted in the books of life, when the world as they knew it was being reformed. Investigations were carried out to understand why humans were placed upon this specific planet. The one called Planted C-53, World and Earth. Intellectuals took to the stage to find the meaning of life and the reasons why this specific planet was chosen for the humans. As with all types of studies, there was a need to return to the source, the creator. The one that brought them out to exist, as they had questions about life. The Creator was to make things clearer, or answer the questions they had. Or so they thought. All evidence point in one direction. The findings from archeological, psychological, ethnographic researches all mentioned the womb-men. She had the power to create, thus they all believe that answers rested with her. The carrier of the egg. As with all other species, able to birth her eggs into life, she had the power of choosing the birth place. Thus, standing in the communication gap between both or all worlds were the womb men. Later called the women and female species guarding the portals of the planet. They served in many positions, which were both physical and spiritual and wavering against others who tried to infiltrate their space while equally praying and nurturing their offspring. During ancient times they were the orchestrators of children birth. It was the duty of the wombmen to decide when a child was to be born as she initiated the entire process. The ancient woman would isolate herself for days, meditating and seeking audiences with the gods for a sign. The sign would always come in the form of a new song deposited privately into her soul during isolation. Once she learns the song by heart the wombmen would then engineer the mating process with the husband and throughout the entire session sing the song to her husband. Each song was child specific and would be the child's identification throughout his/her lifespan. The life bearing songs had the power to open the portals of seven heavens from which the spirit reincarnated to the earth. This could only be attained through the approval and willingness of the egg bearer, thus the legal right to dominate earth was given to the humans. In this case the Creator did not include itself in the legal authority structures on earth. As only spirit in a physical body had access. The gods needed permission to activate supernatural influence on earth, this was granted to the human beings through the women, who was the bearer of the sacred egg. The wombmen, thus had many responsibilities. Systems and tools were therefore needed to perfect the art of their duties and one powerful tool was the power of magic. These women were revered of good standing who held down societal and spiritual responsibility in favor of the advancement of the species on Earth. Yet over time, they were persecuted and their duties were diminished in some parts of the world to worthlessness. They were the Gangas with their worshippers, the Arch Priestess of the Sun-Goddess at the Great Shrine of Ise, The Nihongi, The goddess of Armenia, The goddess Ishtar, The goddess of Wantonness, the Melissai and Claudia, the Minoan priestess, Aphrodite, Artemis, Bellona or Duellona, Mama-Quilla and many more. They were the women standing in the earthly and spiritual realm of the great Planet C-53 embracing the universal presence to make known to its inhabitants the rituals which were to govern them. They were hosting different ceremonies, festivals, and rituals, of which most dealt with life-bearing initiations. As sexual priestesses, they orchestrated love and the divine power of sex. Having mastered the art of manipulating and conditioning men with the seductive skills of sex, they maintain the strings of government.

The planet was created as one. There were no continents, only one people living in one space. However it was later separated into many continents by natural forces. The main parts of the continent remained intact and with a good supply of natural resources become the motherland. This was a continent divided into many tribes, each tribe having functional priestesses taking care of everyday life. Rainmaking was one of the most important activities alongside pro-creation, while one multiplied the people the other did so for the plant and animal kingdom as well as provided vegetation for food security. Rainmaking was mainly carried out by the women and men were not allowed at these ceremonies. The women taking part in the rites were usually naked. They visited the water springs and cleaned them out, then drew fresh water and threw it over themselves. The women were also considered priestesses of the moon deity. As time passed and people increased on the continent, so did their hunger for power. Each tribe was training up their own priestesses and soon there were too many masters leading the people of Planet C-53. They didn't only give birth to females but male presence also increased. The very women, pro-creators and life bearers, strove against one another. The power of control became overbearing and greed stepped in with each woman being accustomed to what they had not mastered; raising sons. Although he had a soft spot for the mothers' heart, he was but fierce in battle and had a mind of his own. He had a domineering mindset with a will of its own. In the quest of raising him as the ultimate force, the women made him the keeper of their secrets and because of his strength, he became the Knight and protector of the Great House of Bulan (Truth). Exposed to the sacred information of Planet C-53, men imagined the powers they could possess, and ultimate authority they could own. They loved the egg-bearer and appreciated the care bestowed upon them. However, their individual mind saw that there was an opportunity to take over everything. They could change the cards because the truth was in their hands. Soon, the men raised by the women, gathered at secret places and re-wrote the laws. They burned the original scripts and started a witch hunt on women and had reset history in their favour. During those times the ancient male had no governing power. As it is today, in ancient times women led in all aspects of life but with the increase of sons, new challenges aroused. The mind of the male was conditioned differently and his nature was not gentle and caring. In his quest for power, the male reversed everything that the women set in place and as a result engineered the birth of anarchy. Although Planet C-53 or earth as it is known today has many continents, in the beginning it was one piece of soil which was named Alkebulan/Aphrike (the Land without cold or horror and a united source of progression and great kingdoms). As the minds of the inhabitants evolved they started explorations under the soil and above with tools they created so powerful to drill and dig underground in search of more information. Having the secrets of the Mother, men knew that there existed a different world which could enlarge their territories. Unfortunately they didn't have the mental information women had to understand certain spiritual things. Hence they miss-read some of the scripts in their rush to gain knowledge. The knowledge would grant them immense power to rule the planet. It entailed processes of mining substances for wealth creation. Governance of all men, would translate in ruling plant and animal kingdoms. There was a good system in place that provided comfort to everyone. Each tribe had sufficient affluence and they could co-exist in peace. The competitive nature of men thus created wealthy empires, through engineering the first trade routes, centers and business models were built to advance the citizens livelihoods.

Alkebulan was a major supplier of gold in world trade during the Medieval Age. It was controlled by the powerful Sahelian empires. They made trading devices such as the Almoravid and Fatimid dinar which were printed on gold. Thus, there were trails mentioned and maps encrypted in riddles of how to obtain more gold. They also possessed a heliocentric view of the solar system and palaecontact with the 3 major world which enabled them to make diagrams of planets and orbits through complex mathematical calculations and develop algorithms that would accurately orient travel routes. Gold then became the major trading commodity and the evidence of wealth and power. They had to dig to find gold, trade with and for it, and later kill and betray even for more. Soon, the gold mines became bigger and deeper. As they journeyed deeper, erosion caused large slits in the soil and the substances holding the soil together started to separate. The world as they knew it started drifting apart as pieces were breaking of in all directions and the water from beneath raised to cover the open spaces. As the pieces drifted apart, some fell under the sea, creating yet another world. The soil shifted all around to create the world as it is known today. The engineering beings on the mother continent found ways to create travel paths and routes to explore more and likewise, those that were cut away from the great continent also left with some parts of the secrets found in the House of Truth, guessing and expanding on the little secrets they had, until the truth was entirely distorted.

Part of the creation myths and text found among the scripts of the House of Bulan mentioned that humans were created by Father-Mother God (Amma) in Alkebulan. However, the mothering being had the greater gifts and abilities which encompassed nature and engagement on more spiritual levels. With psychic powers, she could make decisions and engage astronomy for perfect guidance. Yet, during the witch-hunt, metaphors of God were overtaken by patriarchal systems and with this many evils were introduced of which, slave trade and apartheid was amongst them. Under the slave trade, women were sold to the highest bidder. This was later expanded to include men and children. Those that knew of the treasures of Alkebulan came in powerful forces to rob the continent from its best. In a quest to move everything to the parts of the worlds they were building as their own. The mind and landscape was blackened by the brutality and injustice of slavery and colonialism that smothered Alkebulan women. As they caused the first divide amongst the sons they were raising and with only their spiritual strength remaining, another force took over, it was the fear of their own sons which reduced them to silent homemakers, lusting after their husbands and worshipping the husband men and all his evil doings. Today the soil of the mother continent was weeping. Its inhabitants were in disarray as the once effective system of living fruitful lives was taunted by greed, malice, and miss-governed by those in power. What was once a powerful race, is now subjected and reduced to poverty and illnesses. The rains were no more and the people were copying from the new world powers to better understand their plight. They tried foreign systems and tools to fix their problems, yet, the one thing which had prosperously served them was made evil and as a result, they couldn't function wholly. The ancestors were pacing in the seventh realm in worry. They were sending millions of messages to the children, but the children were blinded by the new world. Shamefully with bowed heads, the ancestors could not commune with the great gods or enter the realms of ever after. For their work has been deemed unsatisfactory. Without completion of the great commission, they could not rest. It was on such a fateful day that Ishtar stepped forth and spoke to the ancestors of the mother continent. She was willing to venture into the atmosphere of chaos and learn their way of life before converting the masses back to the civilized manner which would cater for the rebuilding of its people as they needed a trail to lead them to evolution. With the acceptance of the gatekeepers of Planet C-53, she moved through times and sought an audiences with Ra. Granted permission from all gods and worshippers she traveled on a new quest. She was keen to serve but the condition attached thereto was that she was to start at the very beginning. Traveling to that specific planet which was different from the others meant that she had to reincarnate into a body temple of one of its own. By her spiritual nature, it needed to be a female body as the task at hand required the understanding which was only bestowed to the hosting species upon creation. This exercise could not be executed to perfection in any other body temple. Found near the sea and close to a space where the ocean meets land, Ishtar was lying naked under the foggy air on the damp sand. There was no ounce of shiver and the skin was hot, unlike that of a new born babe out in the cold. Her rescuer was an old maiden from one of the surrounding villages called Swakopmund and another Walvisbay. However, she made the dunes her home to engage in free-spirited missions of solitude, which was something the new day species of Planet C-53 did not understand.   Although she was wise and saw beyond many worlds, they called her a crazy old lady. With a chuckle in her voice, she picked Ishtar from the ground and lifted her up to the sky. "Finally you have heard the cry of your daughter, oh great Amaku!" she shouted to the heavens while holding the child up. "Thank you, for I know the time has come for the adversary to meet its end. I shall make haste and deliver her to the proper station." Ishtar could hear every single utterance from the lady. Their eyes locked in recognition of the one world which bind them. With all the excitement in her to utter back to the female worshipper she identified herself. In an attempt to speak, Ishtar opened her mouth in response to the heavenly prayer but all that came forth was a squealing sound. She was caught off guard and in confusion, she tried again and again. Frustrated that she could not communicate with the lady, she cried and the lady cuddled her while blabbering in an unfamiliar tongue to her.

"Ooooh goodsy whooshy, soon nanna will bring you to the right people. Don't cry my Nani nossi dundla dingi."

Ishtar could only look at her in confusion. Both, herself and the lady knew that this was indeed going to be a new experience for Ishtar and the world awaiting. The only string attached to her and the universe that commissioned her was her spirit. The body temple in which she was clothed was meant to be discovered and atonement found such that they both could exist as one to carry out the great mission.

CHAPTER ONE

Where did it all start? During the great conquest of Babylonian states, the Kings of Alkebulan decided to part from the creator. Setting their own standards of living and making rules befitting the New World. They wanted total control. The body created to house the soul alleviated its own status to Kingship. Trying to control the spirit, which was in conflict with carnal body. The spirit was torn apart by carnal lusts for that which was unfolding in the world versus that which was greater and existed in the universe. It wanted to be part of the new existence and own rights to the earthly revolution. Its purpose was clear to set up a new mandate and create a host that will oversee the new creation. However, the host was tempted to distance itself from the creators and authority that oversee the purpose.

For times immemorial the great continent of Alkebulan was burning with passion. The soil rich in minerals and habitation for kingly offspring. The daughters and sons of the creators ruled with majestic presence. They had the understanding and knowledge that now escape the world. The creators approved their purpose to reinvent and strategically build a new empire and thus they ruled with perfection. Caring for the knowledge and seal of the creators, they engaged in bringing forth masterful improvements to the open plains of the continent. They carved out a beautiful habitat that exceeded the expectation of the third-degree citizens of the universe. However, this achievements turned them into proud beings who walked tall as conquerors, as they developed their little world into a dynasty. Pride blinded the eye and they could not see beyond the evident soil that held their feet. They forgot that a greater service was to be established. This angered the creators and they split not only the language, but also the knowledge from them. The creators hid their secrets in the subconscious mind of the spirit, away from the eye of the host. They flooded the earth with waters and separated it into many different parts. It was known that the creators never backed down from a promise. They created a new species to subdue the earth and promised them longevity, provided they follow the guidelines. Therefore, it was not possible to erase the species entirely from the world created to host them. They had been provided authority over it and thus the creators could not repossess earth. Though the flood separated the earth in sections called continents, they kept intact the mother continent. It needed to exist in whole to host those that survived the first natural disaster. That reference was important to underline the creators' purpose and also illustrate its forgiving nature. With separation, the servant carried away some secrets to sell to the highest bidder in parts of the removed continents. This then created confusion as secrets changed hands from one unknowing source to another.

It was during such urgent times that the call was sent out for a gathering of the seven (7) most influential Alkebulan Empires. The Kingdom of Kush which held the administrative position, had to invite the others to attend the meeting which was to determine the future of the continent. The Nubian empire was one of such that reached its peak during the second millennium B.C and ruled lavishly along the territories of the Nile River like all other kingdoms on the great continent. They traded in ivory, incense, iron and most importantly gold. Gold trading, the epitome of the Alkebulanian dynasty, had the power to ridicule foreign trade. It weakened European money and could afford access that was denied to many others. Kush, along with the Kingdoms of Carthage, Aksum, Mali,

Songhai and Great Rhodesia were amongst the empires that held a golden sphere of power and achievement over the nations of Alkebulan. With gold they had power to reign and create avenues of success. Alkebulan was glowing in prosperity but they lacked the awareness that gold could be traded and either loss or gain its power by exchanging of hands. Equally, they lacked the understanding that it could be a source of destruction. This lack of knowledge created many problems on the mighty soil and it was evident that more challenges were to come. For this purpose and many which the beautiful mothers of the soil saw in the near and distant future, the rulers had to be called and warn. They had to be informed of the best path of wisdom its inhabitants needed to follow and preserve everything of inheritable value. Though the Alkebulanians rebelled against the spirit, they had a strong sense of understanding the importance of observing its powers. They kept the communication channels open and from time to time seek approval from the gods. They knew how to re-open the secret portals through which they could reach the gods. Thus, when the call came through the great Oracle, without hesitance, they knew in which direction to travel. The meeting place was therefore the Land of Punt, known as the "Land of Gods" and the ruler of the Red Sear, which was the oldest and mightiest of all. The power of Punt laid in the hands of womb-men. Unlike other empires of Alkebulan, the land of Punt was governed by very distinguished womb-men. During the reign of Queen Hatshepsut and Queen Makeda, they carried the torch which had to light up the opportunity that elevated womb-men to the power of government in both spiritual, political and economic circles. As a result, degrees made under various ancient times allowed women often to lead powerful, spiritual roles that garnered them respect and admiration from society. They were the referred oracles, spirit mediums, seers and advisors that dominated the spiritual system across the land. Most of them reside in Punt under the guiding pillars of Isis, the queen of all goddesses.

The seven leaders, together with their entourage, traveled from far and near to represent not only their cities but to understand the urgency of the call. It was not every day that the horn of the oracle was blown. It was only during the outmost emergencies that the oracle would come out to speak to the leaders of the land and the last call they had received was fifty five years ago, counting to date. That in itself was extraordinary as the voice of the gods was heard only after every hundredth years. Hence, everyone was worried to be called for an earlier pilgrimage to the mother city of the oracle. Some traveled weeks and others for a few decent days over the vast Sahara and rain forest stretched over miles of beauty that behold surprised rains, strong winds and hot sun. Some travelled upon breathtaking waterfalls and deep valleys while the rest maneuvered camels through dunes of sand which seemed never ending. No matter the challenges befalling them along the journey the mighty leaders trekked over the plateau to reach their destination dignified. They were not rushing because it was well known on the mother soil that rushing always attracted negative forces. With ease and patience they overcame the hurdles during the journey. Yet, they made it in perfect timing, as if they agreed to an appointed arrival time. What a sight it was when they appeared from all seven corners of the soil on horse and camel backs with their entourage behind them. Each adorned in majestic attires that showcased their wealth and culture. It was an expedition of colour and affluence. An expo of high class exodus and before them, laid the village of the oracles, a large oasis with a beautiful scenery. Its entire surrounding was covered with exotic flowers and tiny waterholes spread all around. Embrace in serenity, the beautiful oasis lay in waiting to welcome its guests. The only sounds which could be heard were those from the animal kingdom, of birds singing beautiful choruses and the tiny streams flowing from one waterhole to the next providing agreeable instrumentals. A little swirl of dress material was heard as the queens were rushing about to prepare for their guests. Other than that the oasis was clad in total silence. When all the leaders arrived at the gate, a horn trumpeted through the silence to announce the guests. Everyone, including the musical sounds of the birds, flowers and water came to a standstill.

They all waited in total silence and for the first time in fifty five years, early with thirty five, she rose from her seat and exited the hut. Slowly, with elegance and grace which rose eyebrows in wonder of the advanced years compared to her energy. The oracle walked without aid to the entrance of the oasis. She looked at her visitors with a smile and started chanting ancient lyrics and danced, her voice as clear as day and pure as that of a virgin bird introduced to the mastery of song. After circling them seven times she walked backwards to the entrance before turning towards the east. Without facing any of them she greets them in equal worship to Ra. Only thereafter the maidens and queens rushed over to guide the guest through the gates of the oasis. They all knew that the oracle would engage talks with them at the appropriate hour. Until then, the maidens were to take care of them in all manner, through physical contact as well as the pleasantries.

Usually the leaders would have spent a month or more in the little village, rejuvenating and brainstorming on strategic future plans. However, that night after much festivities everyone retired to their camps, only to be woken by the sound of the horn at 3:50am. Surprised they all rushed to the meeting place where they found the oracle waiting. It was evident that this call was indeed of outmost importance and without much delay, the oracle started talking. "Hail the kings and queens of our mighty land. May you all live long. Standing in the gap between life and ancestry, I bring you word from the wise ones. From the two separate worlds of the ancestors and the gods of our land, a joint message is reaching our ear today. The fall of the kingdom is near and the wise will be blinded by his own ignorance. Your sons will overtake the reigns of the land and step over the womb of the maidens, leaving them barren like the harsh stones of our southern soil. They will sell, not only our belongings but also our dignity because the spoil of the gold will not be enough as their eye will shine a new delight for the white stones of the river beds. Many will be the risen atrocities amongst your sons, weakening and robbing the spirit of the womb-men from her power and exposing her nakedness to the eyes of the hyenas who will scorn her into misery and laugh endlessly. She will fall from grace for many of our million years, such that your homes will be dissolved to nothing and your seeds disappear gruesomely to the ground. You will witness from a far and not be able to overturn the decision from the wise and until atonement has been made. Now today, in the sight of the gods and ancestry comes a divine call to you for atonement for your land. Though the clock has been tight to the perfect hours which came from the creator will happen as decreed. Your land will manifest the destruction caused by your sons, however, through their infinite power of love the gods will give you grace. Merciful grace which is to come to your offspring at the appointed time. You have been called today, to make atonement with the gods so that your offspring will rise above the storms and rebuilt the fallen continent. Your offspring that will be drowning in misery and lack of knowledge won't know what to do on that appointed day and time. Hence, the call for you to stand in the gap for him today in that purpose. The gods will record this day and free your sons because of your genuine prayers. I called you, as such prayer and atonement can only be accepted in the sacred house of the gods when it is done on holy ground.

Your offering of self to become one with the gods will seal a bond never to be broken. This commitment between the two forces will be the only saving grace for the motherland and her offspring. Retire each individual to his camp and cleanse yourself, for the communion with the gods will be at day break tomorrow. You should sanctify your spirits and seek their grace for your land and its people. Although your sons will destroy what they have not build, you need to renegotiate grace instead of total demolition from the face of the earth. It is wise to remember that the first and only habitation of humanity started on this soil. Alkebulanians were not merely an introductory element but great beings with a powerful mission to fashion their existence over the span of the living cycles. It is rather sad that you have all diverted from the creator's plan and now, adversary knocks at the door. Not for today but, to pass during one of the great achievements when you would think that you are indestructible. Go rest tonight, clear your minds and gather at the sound of the horn here again." If they were ever puzzled before, the leaders were now worried more than ever. None has foreseen that a day would come when the oracle would speak to them in the most illogical manner. But they all knew that it was not time for questions yet. The next day, they rose with the sound of the horn. Outside each chamber a maiden was waiting with buckets of water. One of the ponds in the village carried hot water and this was presented to the kings to cleanse themselves. The maidens add herbs into the bathing water which rejuvenate the body and remove unwanted odors from the skin. The kings had to present themselves in pure fashion before the gods. After the herbal cleansing, they were led to another pond, this time one with extreme cold water to dip for a minute. Dressed in purple robes which signifies death, they were led to a chamber of worship. Here the kings joined the queens who were worshiping overnight in an hour long prayer to the gods. When they finally emerged, they were led to the stream for cleanings again and dressed in white robes. Only after that lengthy ritual were they led to the oracle. Her name was Mabel, one of the immortal oracles send by the gods to take care of the people on earth. She served them century after century. Under her guidance many priestesses were taught how to stand in the presence of the gods and serve the people. When they arrived at the great alter where she always commune with the gods, they noticed that she was not alone. Smoke emitting from an unknown source and within the smoke a beautiful maiden stood. "Hail my leaders from the soil. May you live long," she greeted them all, for the first time ever, bowing to their presence. "Your silent atonement has been received by the great ones of the land. I present to you Ishtar, the goddess from the great beyond. She has been tasked to follow through on a mission to rescue, that which you have destroyed through your sons. Her time to arrive amongst you is unknown and such is her identity and depth of her mission. Today she presented herself to affirm that your prayers have been considered favourably. May you return in peace to your respective kingdoms."

For the first time in history, the leaders journeyed into the wilderness to meet the oracle in such haste, just to be caught off guard and left with a message so dark to unravel. They didn't know what to make of it all, but also knew that no one was going to explain its meaning to them as they had to figure everything out for themselves over time. That is, if time was to be permitted. While they were returning to their camping sides to prepare for the journey back, one leader remained, hidden and looking around curiously at the site where Ishtar stood in smoke. He went about slowly, not sure what he was searching for but kept his eyes on the site. He noticed that there was a trail of gold and he bend down and collected some in his hand. It was the purest of gold he has ever seen. With a smile he swept everything up in his hand, covered it with his handkerchief and put it in his pocket. A gold trail; he now understood the message and thought to himself, that their offspring would deplete the gold and fortunes they now have thus, the warning from the oracle. His untrained mind concluded that the goddess would come to earth once the gold is depleted and restore it again. He vowed there and then to always remind his sons about her and be watchful. Just to be vigilant, he will send off his sons to plant houses in all cities of the Alkebulan and other continents. Since they don't know the appointed time, his vow was that generations will spread over all continents with the information he collected here today. As he was backing out of the meeting place the oracle returned and he quickly hide and sat there watching. The oracle who has always been careful to observe her prayers in solitude wasn't aware of the presence of another at the holy altar. She enquired from the maidens that the shrine was empty before coming out. That's why she started her rituals without making sure that the place was empty from prying eyes. The ritual she was to perform was to open hidden portals in all seven worlds so that she could share secret messages with other species. The last ritual was to seek audiences into the spiritual kingdom. The king listened attentively and memorized the short lyrics which could open the portals to the spirit world. The other chants were too complexed for his ear. As the oracle chanted he could see how that world open up before his eyes. Through the Oracle's voice he leant that there were different galaxies and worlds which they could access through reciting certain phrases and he had just memorized one of them. He was sure that the information exposed, would aid him to execute his master plan. When the oracle left. The king came forward and stood at the exact place where she was standing. He chant the short verse and the portals opened immediately. He could see the spirit world and hear what his ancestors were talking. He could also see into Ishtar's world but their voices were mute to his ear. However, that which he heard from the ancestors was enough. He closed the portal and quickly rushed to join the others to prepare for the journey to return to his land. While in her chambers the oracle had a vision. She saw the king standing at the altar and knew immediately that it has been desecrated. She saw how he returned to burn down the village and built a wall around the altar. Year after year he would return to that altar and look into the spirit world. She knew it was time for them to move to another space in time and century. It was sad to witness the first action of greed and deceit. To see that the children of the soil truly lacked knowledge of the important things in life. It was evident that this particular king did not interpret the scrolls in the House of Bulan correctly. If so, he would have known that the rituals could be practice at any place and the chants could serve many different purposes to manifest real energies on earth. Just as the gods foretold, there was the evidence that the children of the soil would die of lack of knowledge. Knowledge which was right before their eyes, which none could decipher because their minds were untrained. That night after all their guests departed. Oracle Mabel called her people together and send them into different parts of the world. They were transported through magic to all the holy cities on earth and those beyond the seven worlds. At the appointed time they will reveal themselves to mankind.

CHAPTER TWO

Things were done very differently in ancient Alkebulan. Before any mayor change in lifestyle, trade or politics, the leaders had to consult the Chief Priestess or Oracle assigned to each area of living for guidance. They needed to walk at all times under the wise counsel of the Mother Goddess and by constant purification of the soil, they had to stay in touch with the source. There was never a need to write down or broadcast the principles of life as each human being was born with an innate ability to communicate with the sources above the sky, on the earth and below the surface of the earth. The intelligence which was never an absences and the presence of God was accessible as the humans were highly exalted. As no human being had reason to stand in hate, there was peace, the type that surpassed all understanding and love was all around and served every living being. The beautiful paradise of Alkebulan as it was created, was a source of joy. The angels of the skies above would wander through its glorious gardens and observe the wonderful ways of men. They were at awe of their own creation as they smiled in the face of beauty and sigh, because that which their eyes could see was certainly beautiful. What came first was the creational bodies that had the ability to co-create. They were men and womb-men that had to create a structure which would enable adaptability for the generation to follow. Tasked with responsibilities befitting their own body structures, one carried the seed and the other granted all the abilities to turn that seed into a life bearing force. Just as in the animal husbandry, the two energies knew how to commune to bring the seed forth. The male figure had no special powers but to eat, hunt and mate. Whereas the female hunts, shares, births, creates, nurtures, trains and release her young to the wild, fully equipped. Never has there been a power struggle as each knew their weaknesses and strengths. The male was never the leader of the tribe. He only stood in a protective sphere over his pride. For each animal type knew its purpose of creation.

Nature was in tune with the ways of its people as the seasons were operating according to its need with the high Priestess knowing exactly when to carry out the rites which would call for the rain, wind, cold and heat while attentively listening to the whispers in the trees to adjust the times that befit the season. Such were the times in the human and animal kingdoms. The female were the fruit bearers, the teachers, the advocates, the warriors and the rulers, each entitled to its source, as ascribed in the spiritual gifts bestowed upon her. Yet they did not regard the male any less for they referenced the one great power he held within his loins. Thus granting him the superior honour of royalty, to serve him with love and honour him a position of might.

Kingship came into being as the female expanded her worship of the power which the male held because he was required to ignite the source within her to generate life. By nature, there was no other procedure and the womb-men had full knowledge thereof. This manner of exaltation was the element which cause strive amongst the species. As they started searching for the perfect male, it was important to know his blood and genotype so as to determine if the offspring would be perfect and in good health. While the warrior priestess was concerned with the physical appearance of her man, the ruling goddess was concerned about his consciousness and the home maker about his strength. Class and sects were thus created and instead of love and, inner strive, competitiveness and jealousy was born as each was trying to find the perfect male to mate and each looking for solutions to divinely master the entire life cycle.

Full of worry, the ancestors looked upon their children. The nations born under such trivial times separated themselves, each under the notion of supremacy. Those born from one clan thinking that they were better than the other. Unity was disappearing and the children sought out ways to hate their neighbor, the offspring from another mother although they were kinsmen, both created from the same soil. As the years went by, the sons of the soil fell deeper into misery of self-hate and, the principles of life were slowly diluted. The ancestors gathered a committee of representatives to seek audience with the gods. The only way for them to assist the children was to inquire from the gods to intervene on their behalf. Allowances were made in the spirit world through commissions with the gods to reincarnate if need be. However, these allowances were not approved frequently as each being was born with instincts to aid them on earth. The sons and daughters of the soil were equipped with the mental capacity to amend their ways, yet chose not to utilise it. Each time an angle was send from the skies, the people rejected its message. Not everyone was ignorant of the things happening on earth and in the spirit world. There were people observing the commotion in silence. They were a group of wise people placed strategically in each space by the oracle with the assistance of the gods to witness what was unfolding. They did not only record the people's history but also wrote down each message brought by the messengers which the people ignored. They would take it upon themselves to write down the wisdom shared from heaven on tablets or scripts. These were the wisdoms kept in the House of Bulan over time, written as symbolisms, parables, paintings and in many forms which could only be deciphered by the wise eye. In an effort to protect the truth, the ancestors decreed that a wise spirit-man would appear unto the soil once in a millennia to interpret and teach the people about matters of existence. However, humans were impatient to allow times to unfold, they tried to unruffled the secrets without seeking for proper counsel and these acts caused a massive misrepresentation of the truth hidden in the House of Bulan.

Far in a distant space. Under the unseen eyes of the Alkebulanians was a different world. One shared and governed mutually by men and animal alike. One of peace and prosperity. One never disturbed by the fickle minded. Counting down over years and years Oracle Mabel was standing in the animal kingdom informing the King of the Animals, how it all started and why it was important to join the two great earthly forces to rescue their habitat.

"My great and dear friend. I greet you and bow to the Great Divine which is within us, above and below the Earth."

"Dear Queen of the two legged beings, welcome to our home. Please accept our love and gently humility." roared the Lion King.

"Today, I come to you in search of support as commissioned by the gods beyond the thousand galaxies. We need your assistance, once the chosen one makes her presence known amongst the people of Alkebulan. She will come to war against the systems of men and against forces of darkness, ignited by these men. During her quest to lead Alkebulanians on the trail of gold, she will witness many atrocities. She may fall into the enemies trap while trying to understand how the world is conditioned. For she will have neither power nor weakness of mind or body. As we don't know if she will be spirit, men or animal. We thus seek your assistance, when the time cometh to be in one accord."

"Hail to you Queen of the People. It can never be in our favour to refuse you support of any kind. Do inform us how best we are to be of help."

"Right now my dear friend and king. We are not certain as to the type of help the chosen one may require. However, we need to establish an understanding and seek forgiveness from your mighty throne for the atrocities done against the great plant and animal kingdom. The children of the soil misplaced their wisdom and in their carelessness destroyed not only themselves but the habitat belonging to all. Please look with me deep within. As we never shared their history before. May you join my eye to see how life was before and why it changed. Only through understanding that, your heart will link with all in the kingdom of animal and plant to once again unite with us. Through your understanding, others will be more open and willing to reunite forces with the fallen ones."

With permission granted the Oracle looks up to the sky. As the sky lights up from extrasolar planets which held the secrets of the universe. She calls forth strength that allows her access to dimension which was before and that which lays ahead in times. Giving access through her gentle eye to the Lion King to looked into Alkebulan as it was transformed from a once mighty Kingdom into the ruins of today. Lush green fields lay stretch out all around the land of the people and animals. Though they didn't share one voice. There was mutual understanding and chivalry on the shared habitat. The mountains stood in majestic form, circling every valley wherein the humans housed themselves. There was joy. There was laughter. Until one day, when the motherland thundered in distress as the first evidence of dehumanisation was experienced in the Northern parts of Alkebulan. The species murdered the Great Priestesses of the Land. Chaos rose as each one tried to outlive the other. The seal to the House of Bulan was broken and those with power captive. They were sold across the seas and the ones living on the other side did not buy only the people but also captured the land upon which they stood. In their hour of greed men became fools. Such that their voice and knowledge was separated by the gods. The Mother Land mumbled in fear and cried out to the gods. As her children war against each other. From the mountains streams of blood flow into the valleys. The once beautiful garden became a dark place of hopelessness. The blood of the fallen contaminating all forms of vegetation. Killing both plant and human. Bringing the great continent to its knees. The lucky few fled in all directions. Away from the Sahara as winds started to blow and create sand dunes. The eye of the mother and her heart could not stand the sight of misery. Weeping with her fallen offspring she stretch her hand out to forgive. The Mother goddess withheld the fury in her heart, and became gentle to the sacred beings on earth. She gave them an opportunity to learn how to survive in the newly created desert. The children of men were equally resourceful and made a great home out of the mighty Sahara.

However, the underlying feelings of greed and betrayal grew and grew. During the summit of the Empires, one named Memnon witness how the Oracle communicated to the great forces of the universe. Though he didn't have the entire truth he gathered enough on that faithful day to start his new world order. Memnon had no sons because his loins were weak. Thus he groomed successors from his company of concubines. He taught them what he knew and employ warriors to build his empire and ordained his own priestesses. Over time his son's became the Knights of Bulan. Responsible to secure the House of Bulan and guard the scripts of knowledge. His conspiracy was to overtake and rule as the ultimate king. He orchestrated a plan of deception to overthrow the ruling priestesses. Memnon had access to the entire planet, manipulating all systems with his influence. He had the money, obtained from the gold he picked up at the shrine of the oracle which never ran out. He also had the knowledge of the spirit world, thus he could manipulate people randomly. During the split of the earth, some people were shifted towards the cold hemisphere and he made use of them to start building his great plan of deception. He gave them power of superiority and misplaced sense of ownership. Filled their hearts with hatred towards Alkebulanians as they felt rejected by the great kingdom. They found themselves out in the cold during a time that Alkebulan was thriving and Memnon used that to plan hatred in their hearts. Conditioned by the spirit of deception they overpowered the body of Alkebulan which was weakened by the wrath of the gods. Women were removed of chieftaincies which was solidified by the colonial rule introduced by the light skinned rulers that infiltrated Alkebulan from the cold worlds. The generations fell and the once powerful Kingdoms collapsed. The Mother Land wept as the traditions passed down through matrilineal lines was distorted. The Alkebulan civilization of antiquity was lost.

Through the eyes of Oracle Mable, the Lion King looked at the fall of the great Alkebulan. He further saw the species from across the galaxies standing up year after year in fury towards Plant-C53 as they called earth. They were getting frustrated. The children of the soil were separated thousands of light years from them but their level of intelligence was supposed to be greater than that off the alien species. Simply because they were favoured by the gods. However, the children of the soil didn't have the slightest clue of how to make use of all that intelligence. Instead they were dancing around it and in the process destroying the one planet which was to be the crown jewel of the gods' creation. Just as the ancestors turned their face away from its own. So did the species of beyond. It was up to the Motherland to seek help elsewhere. Hence the Oracle's plea with the Lion King to join her in support. Oh yes, he saw the great fall of the Alkebulan son. Who thought it was wise to betray the breast that fed him and sold his birthright to his light skinned brother who fled with the secrets of the House of Bulan. Through this one act orchestrated, the fall of the great Alkebulan and renamed it as Africa.

The great master fell to dust. Ruled by the light skinned who are exploiting the soil to supply the House of Lords in the great Kingdoms of Americas, Europe and

Asia. They shipped the natives as slaves, together with proceeds from their mines to unknown countries. The gold became scarce in Alkebulan but increase elsewhere. The black men from Alkebulan was used in many places to work for the light skinned foreigner. They tend to their farms and worked their fields. They took care of their children and cleaned houses. But, what stood out was that they were recruited to fight the wars of the light skinned rulers. Exposed to world wars they knew nothing about. Yet degraded and made out as nothing in the circles of human existence. As the Motherland was weeping, sandstorms overtook the continent. Forcing it into desert lands. The rainforests were dying out and the great rivers stopped flowing. With food becoming scares the people started fighting the colonizers and also fought amongst themselves. Slowly the once great continent slumber in ruins.

The Lion King looked on and slowly understood the reason behind the great fall of Alkebulan. He also realized that they shared the same umbilical cord. Hence, the fall separate not only the Alkebulan men from himself but broke the covenant with animal and soil. It was not by intend but for that reason and in its quest to eat, the hunt against animals began. In the world beneath the Lion King is aware of a different diet, one of fruit and vegetable and understand now, much clearer why enmity was established on the Motherland against men and animal. As he looked through the gentle eye of the Oracle, the great Lion King set a tear for all that was once meant to be holy. For the first time in history, understanding why the Oracle bows before him. Witnessing the great presence which was within him. The same presence within her and recognizing which was greater. He leaves his throne and bow in perfect submission before the Oracle. "My dear Queen of the Motherland. The wisest of them all on this side of the sphere, carnal to the body and holy to the most high. On behalf of the four legged beings, the sky trotters on two legs and feathers, the finned creatures of the waters and the mud dwellers beneath. I bow in respect and adoration for your great knowledge and patients in serving the great commission with such deep commitment and understanding. I hold reference of your humility and faithful conquest for peace. May your light never cease to exist? From henceforth be assured that the animal and plant kingdom stands in support in the quest to make Alkebulan great again." The Oracle also bows to the Lion King and with a grateful heart bits him fare and well. For at the appointed times they will meet to present the conscious world of Alkebulan with its savior. The search for the chosen one has therefore commenced and she was to be more vigilant, waiting and watching, both the stars and the sun as the clues of intelligence was embedded therein.

As she was turning away to return to her own people. Her eye light up again and she look into the distant future. The species from the Planets far and near were preparing themselves to destroy Planet C-53. They were frustrated as the inhabitants of C-53 had lost all reason of law and order. Their technological advancement was out of control and destroying not only them. The ozone layer which surrounds them was slowly damaging under the heavy pollution caused by the industrial substances. Unknown viruses were plaguing its citizens. Above all they built a space war craft which was to prepare for any war fare in the galaxies. The fear of all this irregularities reaching their own planets made them form a united front to attack and destroy C-53. She also saw that at the exact time of the meeting of leaders from foreign planets, the gods agreed to favour the cry of the Motherland. The beautiful goddess Ishtar was being prepared to reincarnate. Into a body temple of a young babe, she was transported by high frequency to a far of land in the South West of Alkebulan. The gods have chosen the virgin land of Namibia. A densely populated land which gained its independence a mere 30 years ago. With only a handful inhabitants, compared to the over populated neighbouring countries. This was the ideal land for Ishtar to study the human race, investigate its governing systems and train the warriors. She would be outside the radar and the busy bubble of the rest of the world. Reincarnated into the body temple of the Nama tribe, which were Hamites mixed with Khoi-San blood. Hamites were descendants of Ham, son of Noah, as described in the foreigners' book. They were a subgroup of the Caucasian race along with the Semitic race in the north of Alkebulan. Over time they migrated to different areas and soon some of them found themselves in the southern parts of the continent. Hamites intermarry with the Khoi-San who were the oldest inhabitants of Southern Alkebulan. The Khoi-San were natural hunters and shaman with the best medicinal and tracking knowledge.   Thus the gods chose wise. The blend between the two races was the perfect conditioning for Ishtar's body temple to infuse the spiritual powers which would enable her to carry out her purpose and communicate to the universe through the body temple just like the Khoi-San people could. The Oracle smiled. The gods were full of humour she thought. Their request was urgent. But true to their fashion, they send a babe. With a sigh the Oracle bowed in a different direction, looked up to the sky and mumbled.

"Very well then, Great Creator, now we wait for thirty more years for this one to mature. If she would be different from the other only you and time would tell. We will wait, offcourse who could be in a hurry now."

Unfortunately, Oracle Mable was not alone. The all seeing eye of Memnon also had a vision. Though his light does not shine into the house of foreign planets, he too had access to the house of the gods. He could also see Ishtar reincarnated, but what her mission was and which powers she had he could not tell. Memnon was not a patient man. He had no interest of waiting on gods. He fought long and wise. Building systems that governed the world in his favour. From the Knights of the Great Seer to the new currencies which control the world, he had strategically placed his disciples to govern. One of the many secrets he discovered was the power of longevity, making him the oldest living being on earth. During the same time of inception of his plan, he build an army able to withstand carnal and spiritual powers. He made a vow not to relinquish power on Earth. This was his kingdom and the reign not to be shared. He was ready even if it meant killing a baby and be the last men to remain standing on the face of the earth. He re-created the kingdom which was not his.

Memnon was one of the first kings of Alkebulan. After discovering the secrets of life at the last meeting with the Oracle. He orchestrated the distraction of social structures as people knew it. From the north to the south, east to west strong winds of change was blown and many succumb at the hands of the followers of Memnon. The spirituality and all forms of divine beliefs were distorted. He took the slow growth of technology and science out of the doors of Alexandria and revamp them into new foreign ownership. Assisted by nature that split the flat grounds of the motherland into many different continents. He was moved with the tights into the most distant of lands. Armed with the secrets from the House of Bulan and the vision of the ancestors of Alkebulan he had the perfect tools in his hand to change the world in his favour. He was not a patient men but planned strategically. After the invasion of other continents. Rediscovering that which has been in existence long before him and changing it in his name. Memnon was able to plant his secrets in parts, all around the world. With overseers from his house, it was easy to control and monitor the growth of his master plan. However, people had the same fickle minds and it was difficult to control. Hence, execution of his plan was delayed. Each servant of Memnon, once initiated into positions of power tried to enforce his own mandate in the country under his rule, though carrying the ring of Memnon, obtained through rigorous training and sacrificial rites which initiated them into the brotherhood he established. They soon formed fraternities to exploit the big plan. Power was deceiving. It blinds the eye of the beholder. And though cloth under deceit, those that willingly served under the leadership of Memnon were human. They were not born of his loins. As much as he tried, his seed was not of the fruitful. Many a concubine rest under his thighs. He mesmerized them with the potion of love and manipulate their thoughts with lust. Yet, year after year, he did not fertilize an egg upon to call his own. Soon he became frustrated which birth only carelessness. The concubines in his house gave birth, to many sons and daughters. They were not his but, of the servants with strength in their loins. They resembled not the black man under whose roof they were born. Though the features of the body temple was the same. They lacked melanin which identified the beings of Alkebulan as a nation. At first Memnon was furious. He wanted to destroy everyone that deceived him. For days on end he mercilessly tortured the concubines to identify the men that stole from his gardens. None of the women spoke and after time his anger subside. When he was at his rest, one of the first concubines that joined his household came to him. Whispering how important the light skinned was to mastermind his great plan. They were, after all, offspring of the same blood, keen of the soil, lightened by the absence of the sun and different foods exposed to them. Through them, she whispered, he could build a race superior and mightier than those in Alkebulan. She thus presented her sons to lead the conquest for him. Memnon was delighted and could not see the deceit in the woman's plan. She too had ulterior motives to position her sons by dethroning Memnon in the future. When the expeditions to the rest of the continents were send out. Her sons were the leaders carrying the tablets of secrets. Made available only to them. The explorers didn't have an easy task as there were inhabitants on all those continents. The split of the great Alkebulan drifted many off in different directions were they overtime either forgot some of the worthy principles taught on the soil of Alkebulan by the wise. Or expand that knowledge in broader perspectives suitable for the conditions under which they found themselves. Though there were physical differences, the general forms of spiritual observance remain undoubtedly similar. Each society, natively found on the continent exhibit signs of worship and lifestyle which had its roots in Alkebulan. Enhanced by practices of the atmosphere and environment they had to live in, the principles were applied. For Memnon's servants it was difficult to convince this strong believers and fought the natives. Soon the first explorers were emerged into the lifestyles of the natives and loss. Memnon was defeated but remain courageous. He agreed that Alkebulan offspring no matter where in the world and with only a portion of secrets from the House of Bulan, still possessed the power to live according to the age old principles and practice. Thus he, resort to the age old trick of manipulation by introducing a new religion. He rewrote all that the people knew and made himself the ultimate savior instead of Amma. Through a disguise of humility and kindness which the natives welcomed as good character. He sent out missionaries to all parts of the world to spread his gospel. Soon his new explorers were received. They taught the native how to speak and read his tongue. Taught them the importance of the book they carried. A book written in the confinements of his chambers referencing the stolen wisdoms from the House of Bulan. He conditioned those inside his house such that they believed each written word without doubt. It was important to have them belief in the contents of the words. Their unwavering belief that the scriptures were true would make it more acceptable to those they share it with. Memnon was wise in his cunny character. He made his stories relatable with obvious references to past events of the black nation, thus it made sense to the reader. The mystery surrounding the main characters resonate with the minds who were used to worshipping mysterious and unseen gods. He further paid archeologist to attached links from their findings to his book. With careful dedication he taught his subjects what the power of belief could do by training them up in magic and showing them places of worship to strengthen his book's content. This was the beginning of teaching preachers to minister and spread the word. After years in close monasteries they were send out to the unfortunate world who were already waiting to meet the divine savior. They came, while the people of Alkebulan were rushing through tough times to understand themselves in the change environment and convinced them of the power of their unknown god. His subjects managed to infest the minds of the natives. While the natives feasted on the new found faith, the explorers secured themselves in the land. Memnon then send in the second forces. These were to bring in unknown diseases to weaken the immune system of the people. Many succumbed to the strange diseases and others were driven to madness and anxiety. After the spread of the epidemics the sons of Memnon would produce antidotes which they had in their care all along under the pretense of new scientific discovery. Pretending to rescue the people from unknown diseases, they could then claim heroism. As the natives were warming to the modern ways of the explorers, a new adoration was born. With the adoration and trust established the third phase was initiated. New rulers were introduced in the land. Only Memnon knew the great plan thus all the servants send forth didn't knew what was expected of them. They didn't know of those coming after them. The missionary didn't know about the doctor and the doctor was not aware of the mission of the engineer. This created internal strife. While the one tried to destroy the other helped the natives. However, theses were part of the great plan, such that the natives could separate and attached their trust to those with good intend. The rulers came in with might, killing natives in great numbers and planting their own in leading positions. Natives were subjected to harsh conditions making them dependable on the good alms of the missionaries. Not knowing that all these strategies worked perfectly in setting the big plan in motion. The people were reprogrammed. They started destroying all that they were and buried themselves underneath a lie. Turning their eye away from the principles of nature and embracing the new religion of the missionary and explorer. No matter under which disguise he came, for they were made to belief that only those with lighter skin were more powerful, wiser and able to create. None of the natives believed that they were able, even though they were the architects, as slaves, who build the new dynasty under which they served.

Alkebulan had many sons and daughters and the lighter skinned were equally its offspring. Leaving the sunny fields of Alkebulan the children went into the far ends of the world, they settled into winter-lands which were so severe that it scorched them. The sun was scares and they lost the strong melanin which was to keep the heat within their skin. These children of the soil became isolated and soon became revengeful. Memnon was one of the few that travelled off land into the distance of separation. This was ideal a time for him to create another world for him and those that followed him. They were thrown back into barbaric lands and had to work hard to imitate the lifestyle they had in the great cities of Alkebulan. Memnon knew that Alkebulan also had other privileges other than the secrets found in the House of Bulan. Secrets which were now in his care. One of it was the slave trade map outlining the routes to the East. He traveled to the east to see how much information they had. Walking around their cities dressed as a trader, he observed what they knew. Not only did they had the same information on their scrolls but also large amounts of gold which they moved from the chambers of their fathers. They also made use of the things taught by their parents and search for their own gold. Having the understanding from the scrolls it was easier for them to move to the far ends of the eastern soil and practice those believes. Memnon however didn't venture into taking them into captivity, which was something he later regret. He spend time studying the secrets written in their scrolls. The secrets were not only of spiritual value but they had blue prints of modernization. Through the scrolls Memnon and his servants started building replica cities of ancient Alkebulan in the parts where they were living. They had to adopt the cold weather. During early days, many succumb to the harsh conditions of the ice, as their bodies were not accustomed to snow. But with the secrets of the scrolls Memnon recreated live in the cold cities. He stretched his knowledge from the scrolls and add his own imagination as he went on discovering more land and people. Being the experienced, different and well-traveled person amongst those that he would meet. It was easy to formulate his lie.   He seemed wiser than many and they believed everything he told them. It was easy to rule over them and so a new dynasty was formed. The same dynasty which would later bring Alkebulan to its final fall.

Though it was hard to be separated Alkebulan also adjusted and continued living and striving. The few remaining on the birth soil were now more manageable and they could spread out all around the continent to search for new land to set up home and live. The Alkebulan race was not one to be governed by any leader. They had the power to govern themselves and knew the importance of aligning with the principles of nature and their ancestors. Thus even through separation they all maintained their culture which was developed more as they traveled inland and discovered new animals and plants. Alkebulan remained grounded under the pressures that separation imposed on them. The wisdoms stolen from the House of Bulan were still fresh in their minds and this time around they decided not to write down the revelations they received from the gods. Instead the instructions from the ancestors and the guidance by the oracle and priestesses were communicated verbally. They hide them in tales which was passed on from one generation to the other. The voice became the greatest source and they would meet around the fire at night fall to tell the young ones about heroic deeds disguised in fantasy. As they were growing in mind and stature, they also made use of new found ideas and rebuild their cities which they were discovering. They entirely disconnected from the animal world. They were no longer equals walking the same space on the soil. The actions of the humans made them superior above the animal. Soon enmity formed between the two as they hunt and killed each other. Aided by the powerful presence of the gods in their lives the people of Alkebulan multiplied and overpowered the animal kingdom. Animals were voiceless thus they remain in good standing with the plant kingdom. Indirectly the humans brought them closer and alienated itself in the process. The animals appreciated the providers of food and treat them with due respect. During that time, Alkebulan also found new trails of gold and other minerals. As they trekked through the barren lands not yet discovered they found that the mighty river of Nile extended from the north to the south and branched out into all directions. They found waterfalls, beautifully extended rivers, swamps and majestic mountains and different more animal species. Because of the enmity created during the early days with the animal kingdom they didn't establish a relationship with the new species of animals but continue fighting them. The new plants they discovered were unknown and wild and in the quest of finding eatable fruits some died. The deaths were a source of concern to the inhabitants of the land and instead they started eating the flesh of the animals they killed in battles and distance themselves from eating plants.

Memnon also a son of the soil did the same, as he was taught by the same hand that raised all the powerful leaders of the Motherland. He explored more land and tamed more animals to bow to him. The ancestors were not happy, they send messengers to the children but only some gave ear to the sound of their voice. Memnon remained distant from the ancestors. His plan to build a dynasty far greater than Alkebulan foiled his existence. He knew that he needed more hands thus build ships to travel across the distant seas in search for more land and subjects. All around him the human race was reforming and building new lives. He was not the only one that was separated but Memnon was wise. He knew that the gods gave them powers enough to maintain a good lifestyle. They had the mandate to establish a world for themselves on the planet just like the other planets' inhabitants were doing, with the understanding that the overall law and order was to be reserved for the House of the Lords. Cannily Memnon changed all that in his scripts. While the people of Alkebulan chose not to write down their knowledge in case it be stolen again, Memnon made use of this knowledge and scribbled every experience on paper. This piece of information became he's strongest allies during the takeover of the world's great powers. With mighty ships Memnon and his servants traveled far and wide. Withstood storms so mighty on sea and engaged in fierce battles with inhabitants of the cities they found. The strategy was to kill the leader and overtake that which they have discovered and changed it into his name. Slave trade was an important and powerful tool to find subjects, thus he engaged in it with all his power. With the Americas and Asia Minor in his power it was easy to build a dynasty which was not confined to one piece of land. By bringing in new forms of believes with orthodox rituals to retrain the mind of the people he built for himself many kingdoms all around the world. Kingdoms that were lost to thought and hungered for a great leader. Humans were tortured and their minds recondition to such extremes that they believed Memnon was their god. The one they have been waiting for many years to see. Simply because of the stolen riches he claimed to own from the cities he exploited.   He opened schools in the cities and taught them new deconstructed laws from his scrolls. Even then the gods remained silent. There was a cry going up to the heavens but the Lords were silent. Perhaps out of shock as they may not have expected their creation to dwell away so far from the truth which was within themselves, or perhaps they wanted to see how far they would take the newly crafted lifestyle. After all those accomplishments abroad, Memnon left Alkebulan for the last. He knew that the priestesses of the soil were extremely powerful thus he invented the witch-hunt that killed many. During his faithful expeditions he laid small traps for Alkebulan. Their decision to track all over the land was to his advantage as he could benefit through the separation and concur them easily. Under the disguise of spiritual workers his servants re-entered Alkebulan and wiped out the worship of Amma and the other gods. He brought new ways of thinking and put enmity between father and son, the mother against her daughter. Now having conditioned the mind of the offspring of Alkebulan in his favour and owning all their gold, diamond and precious stone in the mines, their oil fields and their women. Memnon's dynasty was growing in power. His subjects were ordered to govern the cities of Alkebulan. Modernizing them through faith and building new structures befitting the found lifestyle.

The heart of the Alkebulan son was not at peace. For he knew deep down that he was created for greatness. It was humiliating to bow to another being knowing that he was stealing from him. The son of the soil could not deal with the thought of being owned by another. But the daughters were becoming weak as the sons could not assist them to war against the intruder. The intruder was from the same loins thus he knew their thoughts. That is why he rewrote history to cater for all areas of concern. He knew that the greatest power would lie in their faith towards the gods. Therefore he reintroduced the salvation that came through one deity. He made that deity equal to Amma as he rewrote the priestly history. It was easy to spoil the mind of the one who was hungry and willing to serve for a piece of food. The sons of the soil grew up under pressure and very soon they started revolting against the new systems put in place. The voice of the mother started whispering in the ear of her son as she could no longer stand the shame that has befall the once great empire of the people. She was in bed with the offspring of Memnon thus it was easier to investigate his chambers. But her sons were stubborn. He saw the flitting gold as his price of gain if he could distance himself from the hands of Memnon. Over the years war broke out and one country after the other was liberating itself from the stronghold of Memnon's servants. They were reclaiming their birthrights. However in the quest of setting themselves free they were signing alliances and treaties with people from other countries, thinking that they were supporting the same principles. Memnon was clever, he had set up home all across the world. His movements were always in disguise. He never visited this countries during the initial take over such that they were renamed and governed by his subjects. The treasures of the countries invaded were the only ones send to his champers. The leaders had to remain under his service contract. He was the ultimate ruler and priest that would only be seen during the purification ceremonies of the people. The lie was thus hidden deep in the chambers of the new church which Alkebulan chose to belief in. The perfect place for the perfect crime.

Alkebulanians were warriors and they carried out bloody wars to free themselves from the intruder. They fought with all types of powers they had. But for this freedom to be effected they had to be exiled from their motherland. From within the confounds of the dark forest they battled against the new master. Deprived from food and water, they had to rely heavily upon the support from their fellow women and children to keep them alive. They formed powerful combats and the knowledge of the soil was to their advantage on the battlegrounds. While they were exiled the masters put traps inside the country. They send off the children of the exiled fighters abroad to learn the modern trade. This children were mesmerized by the advancement found in those cities far off and beyond the sea. They experienced new lifestyles and yearned to be part of it. When they eventually returned home to support their fathers in battle, they had new ideas in mind. An idea to win the richest of the country for themselves. To be able to govern their own fields of treasures and mines of natural resources which could buy them the same type of luxuries they had seen in the Americas, Europe and Asia. True to their nature, the sons overcame and won the battles. They started living lavishly and forgot why there was blood spilled for the Motherland. Every day was a celebration of power and wealth. They befriended the enemy which was once ruling them in the name of global trade and modernization. The world was an ouster and they were on the forefronts of a new game. While the sons of the soil were out playing recklessly spoiling the proceeds of the land. Its citizens were dying in poverty. The boys built mansions and married dames from far and wide. The girls on the soil were named and shamed. New mistresses took over the administration of the houses of the sons of the soil. Children were raised within the confinements of those homes. Schools were erected for them to learn new tongues and reason differently. Visitations to the villages and farmlands were elders were still living were stopped as they didn't want the elders to teach their children irrelevant tales from the past. The elders were scorned because of their lack of knowledge of the new ways of life. The war of liberation was thus not the only price to be paid. The sons of the soil completely sold their souls to Memnon. It was thus difficult to alienate themselves from the strongholds of the one that has created the most deceiving system which had placed the entire world in bondage. Memnon's idea was not that of a small minded person. He had a vision so great and powerful. Its ultimate price to be the ruler of the world. He had a mission to convert every belief and every living soul into one. With one leader, if Amma was the supreme creator of the skies above and below. Memnon believed then he could equally stand as the supreme leader of the C-53 and not just Alkebulan. He was thus infiltrated in every government structure and everything good and bad. If the people from Alkebulan succeeded in building modern hospitals and branched out in new discoveries of treating diseases it was because a buying power was ignited through donations, sales of resources and training of experts by him. All areas which were linked to the ultimate money systems of the world were directed to one supreme office were all the treasures were kept. The house of the holiest priest Memnon. The plan was beautifully crafted and woven within many strings thus there was no direct finger that could point to Memnon. He had clues placed all over the world that made it seem like each country operated in isolation. The political manifestos of each country was devised in such a way that the conditioned mind of the citizens couldn't see the master plan behind everything. Memnon had no time, thus the world spin into a wild race against time. They developed new things every day. Things which were at times good for the people's advancement but costly as it was either polluting the open skies or decreasing the societal norms of the people.

The decreasing value of people and their new religion included many things. The concept of spiritual cleansing and sexual practices was one such entity which was misrepresented to manipulate the mind of the people. Normal codes of conduct were broken and everyone had their rights established thus they could do whatever they liked in the name of civilization. As long as they kept the boundaries intact, people could basically do as they saw fit. The need for parental or spiritual guidance was thus made obsolete. Under this new conditions Ishtar found herself in the heart of the little country Namibia. A country fresh out of the battle fields, they were still struggling with trust issues. Many were wronged during the liberation struggle on both sides of the fields. Mistrust invaded the camps of the freedom fighters such that some people were labeled as spies and tortured unnecessarily. The liberation leaders also succumb to the same pressures that befell the leaders of other Alkebulanian states around them such that they signed treaties for foreign aid. The same treaties which would come back to haunt them in the future to relinquish their hold on the seat of power. It was to this country that she was send. In its infancy and very deeply polluted by the minds of Memnon, this was one country swimming under the lost seas of identity. They were deeply divided and there was no focus to lead the country as a whole. The people were more concern about their ethnicity and the progress of their tribes. As there were no proper reconciliation measures put in place after the war. Those who were treated unjustly on both sides harbored great resentments towards those standing in leadership. The leadership which consisted mainly of sympathizers of a specific political party. There were some recognizable progress in the country but at the same time there was a huge lack in equal distribution of resources. People were becoming grumpier as time passed. The system of the rich getting richer and the poor only remembered during election times also crept in to the veins of Namibia. The youth became isolated and the elders disorientated. The young chose to seek healthy thoughts and ideas in other parts of the world instead of their own. They ridiculed the governors and pledged alliances with the foreigners. The country turned into a mini European state far removed from the values Alkebulan once hold dear. But while Namibia was caught up in its own growing pains the sisters and brothers next door were also falling apart. Angola was caught up in a civil war that lasted nearly 30 years with its freedom only found during the same time its neighbouring country was gaining its independence. Such were many states within Alkebulan. Though they may have gained independence much earlier all of them were caught up in civil war or any other type of war. Memnon's plan to divide and concur. He would assist them during the fight of independence by sending one of his unknown servants to rescue the liberation leaders through aid. Then we would send another servant under his control to support the regime holder. Another to instigate the one against the other. None of them realizing that it was the same entity playing them against each other. For all around the world except the few stubborn once who held onto the true scripts from the House of the Bulan. Everyone else belonged in one way or the other to the world reform plan of Memnon. They were just not aware how deep they were captured. Their lives were entirely consumed by his presence.

He changed everything. Spiritual rites were no longer performed as the church took over the lead to free the people from the supposed bondage from their ancient believes. The government took over the reform of all other social interest of the people. The very same church and government all reporting to the chambers of Memnon. People were not safe in either of the two. As they were spirit beings living in body temples it made sense that they would yearn to bow to a higher power for guidance and strength. This was one thing Memnon knew very well and fought hard against with new ideas he delivered to the people. He knew that once they decipher the truth, the hold he had upon them would cease. That is why he built systems to manipulate their minds. He provided many resources for them to choose from. There were religious systems and millions of sects formed. They came in millions, all in search for that great understanding of who and what Amma was. They had different ways of interpreting the scrolls in their care. For most of them the newly introduced version of Memnon made much more sense as it was derived from historical context of the ancient nations. Nevertheless Memnon was not satisfied with only one piece of the pie. He had to have it all. He had to be Amma and this vital essence of how to reach that level was lacking for him to take over the world, if not the entire universe. This was why he needed to find the gold trail which was written in scripture. The last piece of the puzzle was hidden somewhere and he didn't know how to get to it. Over many decades he had follow the gods as they would send one guarding angel after the other to safe the people of the world from their self-inflicted pain. And time and again Memnon would disguise a plan which would have the people fight against their source of survival and destroy it. The destructive ideas were all found in his scrolls and planned strategically in the midst of the old literature of ancient Alkebulan. Hidden back beneath the ground with leads for archeologist to trace it and proclaimed it as truth, which should be included with the other discoveries. Interpretations of the new information was therefore manipulated every day.

This was the new world in which Ishtar was to set her foot and find meaning. She needed to observe all the things and learn to understand the inhabitants better. But to think and be like them was not going to be easy. Unlike them, her spirit was strong and decisive. It was not conditioned by the system though she was placed under protective care as an orphan with no traceable biological evidence. She is a goddess of high esteem. Her role was to serve under the only authority of Amma as the goddess of fertility and war. With powers such as that she could never bow to an entity in human form. Like all little children her awareness of both worlds was very high thus she could discern people and issues better. However, the limitations of the human body temple was frustrating her. Ishtar the little child was very beautiful. Fashioned directly by the hands of the gods she was flawless. Her features were outstanding and her youthful skin glowed to the glory of the gods. With huge, curious eyes that penetrated the souls of those around her, she stole many hearts. Hence, it was not difficult to find her foster parents and placed her in care. She remained an agreeable child and didn't bother anyone with childhood illnesses or unnecessary nagging. She kept to herself and did what was expected, to observe and learn from the human species. To the human eye she was a happy child, always laughing and giggling randomly. They thought that they were doing a good job raising a happy child but on the contrary, she was laughing at their strange ways. Everything about the human species fascinated her and she became a fast learner. As a spirit and goddess she has never been in human form and she was fascinated by it. She kept touching her face, fingers and toes or at times starring at her body in surprise. It was a delight when she discovered the mirror. Four hours on end she would stand in front of the mirror just looking at her features. If anything, for starters she like what she saw and it was beautiful. As she grew up slowly, she became attentive to detail and master the first stages of developing the human body to perfection. But, what she struggled with was the speech. Not that the uninterpretable babbling seemed difficult but because she was afraid to say or ask the wrong thing. Her instructions from Amma was clear, that she wasn't to reveal her true identity before the appointed time. As she was preparing to reincarnate the angels kept singing the same song to her every other day. This fear was her only hurdle as a child but also one that classified her as a slow learner in the world of the humans. At each foster home she was introduced as a happy, peaceful child with low speech development. While some foster parents took diligent care to help her speak, others simply didn't bother. As she continued to grow, her spirit awareness was declining and the human form increasing. With that came the void of being alone. While other children around her had parents she had no human identity to link herself to and she started learning how it felt to be vulnerable, lonely and alienated. She yearned for a normal home but this was not meant to be.

CHAPTER THREE

Ishtar has been moved from one foster home to the next. No one bothered to explain the reasons to her. Perhaps she was not meant to get attached to people or learn to appreciate the language of love. Each home was, in fact, different than the other. At least they kept her name intact. Ishtar, she was called. No one could tell its meaning or even ascertain her birth date, place and parents. As by the words of the social workers, she could have easily dropped out of the sky. They told her that she was found, nicely wrapped in a beautiful blanket at the front steps of an orphanage. No details about her background except for an envelope which had a white feather inside. In a society expected to care for its young, she was found without home or family and no traceable roots. Yet no one bothered to find out. She was a child like any other and needed shelter, food, clothing, and love. According to the government papers, the first three (shelter, food, clothing), she got in abundance. The question of love and being wanted was what has kept them moving her from one family to the next. As each home she was posted to, had one or the other problem. Thus there was not much Ishtar could do. Quietly, she allowed them to plan her life for her. There was no use of shouting and rebelling. It was worth sitting around in silence to observe the lifestyles of those called masters of earth. Their speech was unintelligent. They eat more than anything other species. Every time she turned her head, they were chewing on something. She wondered why they could not find anything productive to do. Out of a full day, they deposited good hours on eating. The time which would be useful in building their minds for the future. Did they even have a mind? she wondered. They seem to be very busy physically. Yes, yes. They were the bigger ants. Yet they store food inside their bodies instead of storehouses. The only time they were productive was when they were building devices and machines which would destroy their homes or the atmosphere.

Over the past 10 years, she was sent from one foster home to another and learned different ways of living. It proved to her that the species were very different in behavior and lifestyle. They had a complicated authoritative structure, whereby the husband was the head of the home yet everyone listened only to the wife, including the husband. The elders were labelled as the wise and powerful but she learned that the children were, in fact, more powerful than their parents. She learned that the kids were free and powerful only until the age of seven and them something drastically changed in their minds. Her first experience of this phenomenon was at the second foster home. When she arrived, there were already four children. Three of which they called teenagers, who were empty heads. Always nagging about something, eating and yelling at each other. They had very strange behaviour and did not understand the principles of communication. The eldest daughter shut herself out of life entirely. Her ears were plugged with a noisemaker with loud vibrational sounds to which she moved rhythmically. The second one played sounds on an instrument they called a piano and loved cooking. She always had fun cooking with her mother that was infact the only time real laughter was heard in the house. He did not know whether he was coming or going. He didn't speak to anyone in the house unless called directly to attention. Yet he was full of noise outside on the streets with his mates. The poor parents looked worn out. Not knowing how to keep their family together. On top of that, there was pressure from sources outside which they referred to as work, salary, debts, gangs, hospitals and the government. Ishtar did not understand why they could not distance themselves from those sources. Where she came from, there was serenity. You had a choice to shut away from something you did not like. However, these people seem to enjoy the bad things and keep complaining about it. It was a crazy mess. The smallest addition to the house, fortunately, was enlightened. He could communicate with Ishtar in silence. They did not need words to understand each other. In fact, the words they used were also not understood by those teaching them how to speak their language. It was frustrating when you ask for water to drink and they make hot drinks for you. Or laugh with you while you are actually laughing at their random responses to your babbling. Ishtar could thus report with sincerity that the creatures from C-53 were dangerous to the universe because they did not know what to do with themselves. Let alone how to master the space given to them by the highest authority. And yet she was there to find out why and install remedies were possible. Where and how was she to start? Luckily the old people at her first home were patient enough. In their care, she learned the basics of walking in the clumsy body temple and eat the funny stuff they cooked. Very soon they realized that she was drawn to raw vegetables and fruits. This she got in abundance. Why the abundance of the things they needed the least, she wondered. Instead of filling their bodies with water and herbs while rejuvenating their minds. They did it backward. She always wonder whether they know that the largest percentage of their body was in fact water. And they slept for hours. Surely, she was sent to the wrong planet, she argued sometimes in her mind. What was she meant to do here if everyone chose to sleep at odd hours during the day? Calling it siesta and again at night, explaining that the body needs eight hours of rest. This child's body she was hosted in received a lot of spanking whenever she refused to sleep. Thus to avoid the pain and confusion that came with it, she did what they wanted at all times. The babbling babies were usually in agreement with her, and she decided to find out why they were different from the older species.

At the second house, her answer was revealed. When the little boy turned seven her intelligent friend was sent off to a base they called school. The first days were exciting as he was making new friends and discovering things they didn't do at home. But attached to everything, there were rules. He needed to follow each rule as prescribe. This was called societal norms and basic good manners. Thus there was no need to ask why the rules had to be followed. As it was prescribed, so they had to do, without questioning. She learned that adults were never questioned and their favourite phrase words were "Do as you are told."

Thus erasing any sound idea from a child to do what he/she wanted to do. The toddlers begged to differ but it was not their call. For the first seven years, the kids were trained on how to do what they were told and follow rules. The parents were happy and clapped hands for each achievement. Then the frustrated kids grew up and attended high school. A place where they were taught to think for themselves as they were maturing. They were told that oneday they would be adults, thus high school was the training camp of adulthood. By then the future generation of Planet C-53 was completely ruined. They didn't know how to think and be in their own skin. As the elders were dying out slowly, the young just copy and followed in the order in place. Nobody dared to ask questions which would upset the system. The thought of dwelling back into their source for guidance was scary as society has labeled enlightenment evil. In such a world Ishtar was placed and she was to rescue either herself or the people.

Looking at them from a child's view she didn't think they needed to be rescued, and besides those on other planets didn't want them thus they would be better off destroying each other in their personal space she thought. She had information that inquiries were done from other planets when they were looking for a suitable candidate to do the work, every single one declined. Even the gentle

Aguni and the Four Seas have grown beyond measure and they were seeking a new kingdom for their sons. Lutima has broken relations with other beings of the Great Space thus her own planet was excluded from the mother body until atonement was done. They search far and wide and now looking at their messed up habitation and lifestyle it was understandable why other planetarians didn't want to associate themselves with C53 and its people. But, one day there came a rescuer out of a different space. Form the aisles of Ganga and Ephraim, Ishtar was the only one available to remedy a lost tribe's hope to life ever after. When she heard the devastating cry of the motherland and looked into the chaos unfolding, she present herself to help the species. She tought by offering herself, she would be allowed to come in her personal powerful form and do whtat was needed within a split second. Her powers where mightier than most goddesses thus she trusted herself for the mission. Great was the surprise when she learned after taking an oath that she was to go in human form and not just a human but a baby who was to learn for many years how to become an adult. She was devastated but having taken the oath to serve, she could not turn back. No one ever lived to tell the tale if they broke an oath which they made before the presence of Amma. With all those frustrations hidden in her, she took up the mission. And now looking at the people, all those frustrations came back. She was torn by regret of taking up the mission and her fear to fail before Amma. She didn't understand the logic that drove the species because she didn't allow herself to be part of them. Would she succeed if she didn't understand why they were destroying themselves? Never in the world of the gods was there ever a creation that destroyed itself. This was the first of its kind. Over the past 1000 years, they have toiled extremely well on this piece of dirt, building infrastructures of might. Tall buildings with architectural excellence, and strong engineering base that could last for centuries but they tore it down through war and strive. Instead of learning from the structural components of those before them. They became lazy and slack on development, living robotic lives with no vision. They journey to the great land of Egypt to take pictures near the pyramids which were their best achievement to date as a species. If their minds where opened, they would have heard the voices of the Pharaohs, or even took out time to study why such divine works last thousands of years. Instead, they took pictures, ride camels and consume food they label as foreign, simply because they haven't tasted it before. The ways of the alien species on this side of the galaxy was hard to understand. Ishtar looked at them in wonder. Asking her spirit guides what they could possibly have seen in this species that needed perseverance. Given the opportunity, they would infiltrate the order of space and destroy that sole mandate which kept everything whole she thought.

There was one thing though which they seem to understand very well though, and that was the power of mating. This was intense. Engrave in their hearts, that it created havoc if not tended correctly. This was her territory and she smiled thinking about it. Instead of advocating the power of intimacy those that understood manipulated their brethren with it. For countless centuries men had the upper hand in changing the order of life. They mastermind a plot that would keep the women dormant. Studies and concepts were created to make women understand that their existence was merely to serve. They were taught to bring forth the child. Nurture and train it and release it into the care of men. Men who were once known as the weaker species in the entire universe, for they lacked the gift of procreation. They were now elevated to stardom, and given the status just beneath that of Amma. The exaltation of men, in their immortal being was placed above women and the angels. With that all structures in the earthly system pushed out women and centered it on men. They were not designed to lead, let alone communicate to the worlds above. Yet in one single stolen moment of wisdom, grabbed by luck. They twisted the entire arrangement and build a new regime upon a lie. Everything that women were believed to be, they literally burned down to ashes.

Ishtar's eye flashed back into times when churches were created. When the warrior womb men were prosecuted. She looked into the flames that killed many priestesses as the word was distorted to make her out as evil. The yearning of power which laid in the womb of a female, made the men turn vicious. He wrote new laws, structured new religions and build new political regimes to rule C-53. Making it out that C-53 was the only livable planet in the universe and that there was none better than their species in the world. To understand how they did it all, was to understand the weakness and love of the women for that which she brought forth in life. Her own seed created enmity against her. Thus the only source of help needed was to come from the world beyond. She had the only key to call out for help. It took millions of years, as tears have flown on the soil of the Alkebulan dynasty. As the women cried out in desperation. The lords of the universe heard each cry but knew that giving power and lending help would not be sufficient. As the motherland was wounded and rendered powerless. She had to find new ways to return to herself. She needed to learn how to forgive her sons, how to love the unlovable and how to restore Planet C-53 to perfection instead of breaking it down in her hour of wrath. The quest was to restore it to its perfect glory as the divine plan was before times. When the time was ripe Ishtar was released. Not to sweep clean but to build a new rescue team that would guide her in understanding their ways and show her what they required. Her powers were thus needed only to gate-keep and act under guidance as they move towards their perfect destination. At that hour Ishtar realized that she was sent to look at the earthlings through their own lenses and guide them. She was not to guide or war as a goddess but instead serve them with love, the same love that parallel the mother's heart which call out for help. She realized that only such love with patience and understanding was possible to tend to the broken souls of the people and restore their dignity.

While trying to figure out the species she was living with, Ishtar too was growing. She learned yet again that rules were changing with growth. When she became a teenager, she was taught not to play certain types of games with boys. To wear a certain type of clothing, to speak in soft tunes, when to laugh like a lady and even how to address her elders. Having mastered the art of obedience she became a model daughter, a lady groomed to perfection. With her beauty and poise she turned heads where ever she went. People constantly complimented her on her look and classy style. But, she learned that not all could be trusted and kept to herself most of the times. Though she didn't realise it at the beginning her distancing from people made it difficult to know them because she didn't have friends to talk too. The only people whom she would speak to where her periodical foster parents and siblings. This was short lived as she stayed with each family only for six months. For reasons she didn't know at the time, it was divinely orchestrated that she doesn't get too attached to a certain family and move from house to house. But as a teenager it saddened her heart because she could not attend school and be like all the other girls. She would sometimes yearn for their friendships and in the confinements of her room mimic the things she saw them do and try to speak like them. Surrounded by people who seemed to genuinely care about her but couldn't keep her for unknown reasons, she was extremely lonely. Wishing to take part in the girlie gossip she used to hear about, have sleepovers or simply just be a child. Though in the body temple of a child she completely missed out on the experiences of being one. She was more confused as the things taught at one foster home was made redundant by the next. The final, family home before the social service made a decision of sending her off on her own was the worse of them all. The father was the perfect picture of manliness, love and responsibility which the society classified him to be. Reference was made in church, community, and workplace for all other men to lead an exemplary lifestyle like his. He had the perfect family, perfect job and perfect titles. He was handsome and had a beautiful wife and children. They lacked nothing as he managed a lucrative business or two. He was also responsible for the new cultivation of the new mining industry in the country. Every young boy aspired to be like him, every young woman dreamed of a husband like him, and every mother wanted him as a son in-law and creator of her grandchildren. Ishtar could not understand how vein and common the species had become but she had no time to explore them better. Her stay at that house was to be very brief. She had only two months to live with them while the social services was trying to find a job and an apartment for her. They assessed her abilities and decide to settle with domestic work. She proofed to be very neat, cared for little children and cleaned houses to perfection. As the slow speech as an adolescent classified her she was omitted from normal education. When her foster parents inquire about it they were simply dismissed with senseless excuses. So she found herself at her final destination before stepping out in the adult world without a proper home training or education. At the tender age she was to become yet another statistic in a fail system of governance. Two nights prior to her departure the father came to her room. She looked up to him with the same admiration everyone else did. He was always good to her. Bringing her gifts and treating her like one of the other children. But that night, dressed only in a robe he came to her room. There was something different about him. He came in, stood by the door starring at her for a while. With a soft reassuring smile and he came closer to her bed. Then he started to stroke her hair and face while whispering in her ears that he loved her. She was puzzled by his words because he has never been that familiar with her. His actions quickly changed into that of an assuring, caring dad and she relaxed. He said that it was their night to know each other and play a different game. A game she was not to share with others in the house. He lift her up from the bed and started undressing her slowly while dropped his own robe. Not knowing what sort of game this species would play with each other in this form, she remained standing, watching. He touched her breast, caressed her body and moved trails with his fingers across every part of her body. Known feelings were rising up in her body and she was slowly heating up. Her spirit was lighting up small remembrances ignite by the touch of his hands for she was infact a goddess of sexuality, trapped in the little child's body. The child's body didn't understand what was happening. Didn't understand why it was feeling the way it did. He made soft sounds that were tantalizing to the ear. She was not sure whether to like it or hate the acts he did. With confusion, she watched him in silence. Then slowly he dropped on his knees, all the time touching and caressing her. She just stood by in bewilderment. Why was she feeling so uneasy, yet funny excited? Looking forward to experiencing the new game but also afraid. She did not know where the fear was coming from as the mind was closing off all reasonable thought. He slowly parted her legs and caress the insides of her tights. The rush of heat through her body was overwhelming. Then he touched her right in the center of her being. The flood gates opened and she welcomed her new presence with ease. The man saw her transformation and became excited. But he was well advanced in the game, or so he thought and decided to take it slow with her. He knew that she was inexperienced. He needed to be gentle. Get her all worked up to yearn for him in such a way that they both would enjoy the game. He continued touching her and slowly caress her womanhood. Opening her up to receive the volcanic explosions her body was sending through her veins. She started moaning softly and he whispered to her not to make noise as the game was their little secret and he did not want others to hear them. He opened her legs wider and brought his mouth closure to her thighs. With strong hands, he held her up and started kissing and licking her womanhood. As his tongue moved around her privacy, her body went into a rage with feelings exploding all over. Ishtar became at that moment. The man could sense that she was now filled with emotions and at the place where he wanted her to be. She was now in his control. He could do whatever he wanted with her. Slowly he pushed her away from him. With a sudden shock, she looked at him and tried to understand what was happening. He picked her up and move towards the bed. Put her down slowly and covered her with blankets. Her body was shivering, wanting something she could not describe. She lay there perfectly tucked in and not knowing why. The father of the house left her high and closed the door behind him. Living her in a dark room and confused mind. This, was the game that she was not to reveal to anybody? She thought silently. The one to be kept as their little secret? She laid there in total silence. Disturbed by the thought that a respected father would violate his daughter, keen or adopted in such a manner. Slowly it down to her body that what he was doing could not be a pleasurable act. Her spirit confirmed that it was a repulsive act to the body of a child. Exposing a child to feelings reserved for adulthood. The spirit within knew that the act was seen as a reproductive and entertainment form for the humans though it meant much more to the evolved spirit and sexuality goddess. It was also aware that what the father was doing to the child was pedophilia and punishable according to the laws of the world. But the young body temple exposed right there didn't understood any of it. And so would a normal child that was not possessed by the spirit of Ishtar. Anger spread all over Ishtar and she started glowing. Her first time to reveal who she really was. At this stage it was not expected that humans would degrade to such levels to defile the innocent body and minds of the new generation. But at the same time she knew that the rage she was feeling had to mellow down and kept in control. It was not yet time.

Ishtar had a mission, so she let him be. She lay there in the bed so that her body could normalize and after a while she slide out slowly. Dressed in total silence, and opened the door. Eager to learn what the man was up too. She tiptoed to the parents' room. There the mystery was unfolded. Her foster father went to the bedside where his wife was sat in tears. He placed his hands on her shoulder and whispered.

"Now I'm ready for you, come my darling wife"

She tried pushing him away but he was stronger and held her tight. "Do not fight me, dear wife, you are enjoying this as much as I do. Just come to me. And be grateful, you now have a new assistance that can be of good use for our foreplay." He said laughing.

The woman did not utter another word, instead she gave herself to him in full obedience. He was in total control ridding/exploring her through the tears and pain she was experiencing. After a good ten minutes he fell off from her body exhausted and moved in behind the sopping woman to sleep. Ishtar slowly stood up from her position and turned around to walk back to her room. Not knowing that the woman inside saw her.

The next morning the house was awfully silent. As she came into the kitchen everyone was watching her in silence. She sat down and had her breakfast. No one said a word and they all eased finally into their normal self. It was silently confirmed that everyone knew but no one was going to name what happened last night to her. Ishtar wasn't sure whether that meant that she passed the test or not. Seemingly, she was now accepted as one of them. Thus life had to go one as given. The father came in later, jovial as usual. Greeting and teasing everyone. Talking about this and that. He did not eat breakfast, in fact, he hardly ate at home. After a sip of coffee, he kissed his wife on the forehead and left. As the kids were preparing to go to school the mother pulled Ishtar to the side.

"Please, do not say anything to anyone please I beg you. For the sake of our lives, please don't say anything about last night to anyone."

Ishtar was still confused since the previous night and she looked the lady in the eyes while asking. "Is it right? Is he supposed to do that to me?"

"No, my dear, no he is not. But please, please don't let anyone hear about it. Please consider our reputation, consider what people will say about me dear." The woman started crying but Ishtar simply walked away. Thinking why someone should be allowed to violate another being and be protected in such a manner. Perhaps this was the mysteries about the species she was to unravel.

The following night she was expecting him. The woman's plea and the look in the eyes of the other children confirmed to her that what he did was not merely a once-off occurrence. He was to come again and again. That night, however, she was ready and waiting. When he entered the room, she was standing in the same place as the night before. She had no clothes on and ready for him to do what he needed to. Surprised at first, he went in hesitantly. He noticed that there was something off about the girl that night. She was looking different, a bit matured. He quickly dismissed the alarming thought and went straight to her.

"I see our little angel understands and appreciates the game now." He whispered as he started touching her. However, that night was not to be his to call the shots. Ishtar overtook him immediately and he went into a trance. She consumed his mind and create an illusion that seemed real to him. She seduced and teased him in ways he never knew existed. She played the game of love in such a way that it made him scared. For a moment he was bewildered by thoughts. How could she even know the things she was doing to him? He wondered. He had no hold on her, let alone the power to resist her. By then Ishtar was glowing like a star. She did not touch him once. Her mind was the one igniting all the feelings in his body. He was moved from ecstasy to ecstasy. Confusion, pleasure, and lust were all streaming through his body as if on call. She kept him busy for good thirty minutes before his moaning and groaning turned into desperation. The kids in the rooms nearby, as usual, were either asleep or others had permanent headsets on their heads not to hear the midnight escapades of their parents. They all thought it was their parents doing the usual, but this time it was coming from another room. At first, the mother was sitting in tears as usual. Thinking why she kept allowing her husband to violate the children this way. Her parents wanted her to marry him. He was their savior out of poverty, their ticket to wealth. She kept silent because every time she tried talking about his weakness her mother would tell her to endure. That was part of being married she would be advised. She couldn't conceive, hence her husband decided that they adopt. She thought he was loving and caring and agreed. Until she learned of his ill practices. Not only about his in-house sexual escapades but also his infidelity and mall practices outside. Including corruption and money laundry. He was deep into everything he did and blamed her for his lack of the one or other. Conditioning her mind with fear that she would equally be held accountable if he was ever caught. She loved the kids they adopted dearly but every single time when they turned thirteen, he would sodomize them. It did not matter to him if they were male or female. Heartbroken and powerless she would look on and turn a blind eye. Her turning a blind eye caused a rift between her and the kids. Such that they also started using her only for their benefit. Be it for money or just a means to an end. She knew that they too have discovered her weakness and use it against her. When social services presented them with Ishtar she noticed something unusual about her. By simply looking in her eyes she could sense that the girl was different. There was genuine love shining from her eyes but also something she couldn't place. She knew intuitively that the new girl would either be a savior or destroyer. However, that night hearing the noise from the other room she was not sure. It seemed as if the girl overpowered her husband's lust. Instead of just playing with her as he did with the others it sounded as if he was going all the way. After a full hour, she couldn't bear it anymore. She marched straight to the room to confront her husband. When she opened the door, she found her husband curled up on the floor, crying, groaning and moaning. Calling the girl's name over and over while getting one painful orgasmic experience after the other. She was shell shocked at first but recovered quickly when she saw the glowing light which surrounded the girl who was sitting in a peaceful position a good distance from her husband. She quickly rushed to his side and pulled him out of the room, while yelling at the girl.

"What the hell are you doing to my husband, you witch!"

Immediately at the voice of the lady, Ishtar regained composure. The light disappeared and she collapses to the floor.

The lady pulled her husband out of the room and rushed back inside screaming to the girl.

"You witch, get out of my house. Do you want to kill my husband? What sort of black magic did you use on him? Get out now!"

"You said what he was doing was not right. Was he supposed to keep doing it?" Ishtar asked confused. "You did not like what he was doing. Why allow him?"

The woman was completely derailed by then. "You witch, I did not ask you to help. Get out. He remains my husband. Get out!" she kept yelling. By then all the other children came rushing in to see what was happening. Their father was curled up naked in a corner outside the room while Ishtar was yelled at. The angry mother started throwing Ishtar's clothes out of the window while screaming to her to leave their house. Ishtar sat silent for a while then stood up and started walking out. One of the girls hold her hand in the corridor and whispered softly. "Thank you, someone had to deal with him. Thank you." Then she let go of her immediately.

Ishtar did not collect any of the clothing thrown out, neither did she stop to dress, she just walked away into the dark night. Ishtar walked that night through the streets of the capital city. Their house was in the black community called Katutura. A place loaded with profound history as the people of colour were forcefully moved from conducive environments by the colonial masters to live in harsh condition in that space. Over the years this location was developed to meet or at least cater for some of the needs of the people. Today it is a blend of sophistication, luxury and also of hardships and struggle. It has expanded beyond the space of the city center and all the new leadership at one point lived in that location. It had its affluent areas but also some sections were people needed to think twice before venturing out at night. Ishtar had to walk through all those streets alone. Without money, a relative to call or a place to call home. All for the quest to free the people who were stubborn to adhere to Amma's commandments. She was lonely but not frightened, didn't know where she would sleep that night but wasn't worried. However, as she walked alone through the streets, she cried for the earthlings. If some of them had such great power to destroy a child's life the way her foster dad did and the mothers not able to stand up for their children, she didn't want to live in such a world. She cried that night for every innocent child birth by this species and left out in the degrading systems. She cried for lack of love and care. And at that very moment her strength was restored.

Just before day break she met a couple of street children rushing by her as she entered the city center. Instinctively she followed them closely and soon found herself under the infamous bridge in the city center where all street dwellers housed themselves. She watched from a distance how they were preparing spaces to sleep. From the river bed close by they brought worn out blankets and made their beds. Some of them just slept on card boxes. Ishtar moved closer and sat at the far end of the bridge. Watching and waiting before she would be comfortable to sleep. She had nothing with her. No clothes, no money thus didn't fear being robbed. All she wanted was shelter and she knew she would get it in that place. Later as she was about to drift off to sleep a tiny hand pad her on the shoulder. She looked up in the most adorable dirty face of a boy. He smiled broadly and held his hand out for her. Silently he led her to his corner and directed her to sleep on his little matrass. For the first time Ishtar received unprecedented kindness out of the actions of a child, possibly not older than 10 years. She laid down and watch him cover her legs with his tiny blanket and position himself on the ground next to her. That little boy watch over Ishtar the entire night. The next morning he introduced her to the other kids. They didn't ask unnecessary questions, only the name of the new addition and that was it. It was common that from time to time new members would join, some would stay long, others just for a few days and disappear. The reasons why they came was not important and the only rule was to be protective of each other and hustle on your own. Their lifestyle was different and all they cared about was survival. Ishtar was thus accepted and introduced to the streets by her new protector. Though there were tough times out in the street, this was the happiest time in her life. Finally she had friends and people that genuinely cared about her safety.

CHAPTER FOUR

Today, the experience in another set of the world has awakened her spirit to question her birth. She needed to know who she was and what her purpose in this weird circle of life was called. Thus far, moving between one experience to the other, being swift mentally and challenged on spiritual levels. She could not make out who she was. There were fractions of it. Times were she knew that she had extra celestial powers and other times she was simply human. By standing with the street kids she was exposed to the brutality of live as it was seen from another angel. Yes, there was the good but hidden beneath the good was the harsh realities of life that not many talked about. She saw through the lenses of a street child just how cruel the species could be. Saw their selfish acts and midnight escapades. Witness the plots discussed in the night's shadow by men and women in elite positions. Witness the horrors committed by trusted citizens and people of good standing in the work place, fine houses, religious groups and all. Ishtar realise that the streets were to be the training ground she was being prepared for. Here during the midnight hour, everybody stood in the presence of the naked truth. All that they cover up during the night was witnessed by those without shelter. But they didn't have a voice to speak as the society during the day was highly alleviated and the street dweller rejected as scum of the earth. That very place with its challenges was the shape swifter of Ishtar, as she became to unfold into her purpose. She had weird dreams that would transport her at night to odd places. Passing through spiritual portals and engage with people she didn't know. There were random messages and hints thrown her way and she was certain that it couldn't be ordinary. When she told her new friends about it by day they would simply laugh and call her a witch. Some would even justify that she was a friendly witch. Deep within, it was clear as daylight that her life was much bigger than the ordinary. Passing through the portal was a mere fraction of who she was. Yet, the answers remained distant. As that night she was moved to yet another dimension to uncover her identity.

By now Ishtar has been on the streets for nearly a year. She was laying peaceful on her matrass when she heard screams and running footsteps. The little boys with whom she started out were safely in a children's home by then and she was alone. There was no time to ask questions. They all knew that a scream was a sign for each one to save his own skin. You had to hide first and ask questions only when the danger has passed. Unfortunately Ishtar was slow that night and was caught by men dressed in black. Together with other girls she was bundled up in a truck and driven away from the bridge. The truck drove all night and by day break they were in a disserted empty road and space. The drivers had to make a pit stop and the girls were also allowed to come out of the truck. They were allowed to stretch their legs and provided with food and water. Ishtar was trained by her street friends to always sleep with a tiny backpack in which she kept bare necessities. They were accustomed by police raids, gangs harassing them or even human traffickers ambushing street dwellers, thus they had to be prepared. The smugglers were heavily armed and knew the girls won't be able to escape easily thus they gave them liberty to leave the truck everytime they stopped to rest. They had to make the trip look like a joy ride instead of a trafficking in case other cars drove by. Ishtar look around her and saw the beautiful landscape of the country stretching out before her.

From afar, the sand dunes look inviting and capture the adventurers' eye, she knew immediately they were heading for the coast. The dunes stood tall glimmering like gold in the hot summer's day. There are no footsteps and it was void of any human contact. Perhaps it has not yet been discovered by the many adrenaline and adventure-seeking beings who travel to the coast each year to relieve their hunger. Then again, would they she wondered, because many people do not use the hidden off roads that lead to this part of the country. She looked at the dunes as they stood like mysterious Egyptian pyramids. The wind silent and slowly running through the dunes. Just touching the top like a mother caressing its young. Ishtar looked at it in wonder. The journey was long and tiring. They started out through the Khomas Hochland which is a part of the interior plateau of central Namibia. To get where they are without sounding the alarm the traffickers use the C26 route which was probably the most spectacular and interesting road. It goes from Windhoek along C26 via Gansberg nicknamed "Namibia's Table Mountain". This is the longest and the highest pass in Namibia. The name derived from a Nama word "gan" meaning "flat on top". It's one of the highest roads in the country. The pass is traversed by the C26, a gravel road. The flat-topped Gamsberg is part of the Great Escarpment that separates the Khomas Highland to the east from the low-lying Namib Desert to the west. The route travels through the southern regions of the Namib Naukluft National Park, and it will lead you all the way to Walvis Bay on the iconic Namibian coast. The drive is rough on a mostly gravel road. The unpaved sections of the road can be impassable when wet. After the rain, sections of the road can become decidedly hazardous when fast-flowing creek crossings and slippery mud can cause road closures. The pass is one of Namibia's most popular passes and it is, in fact, the highest and the longest pass in the country. Its elevation and the fact that it overlook the Kuiseb River in the valley below it make it one of the most scenic 4x4 routes you can travel on in Namibia. The road is a far more scenic alternative to the traditional route along the tarred B1 and B2. The pass takes adventurers passed several abandoned mines and houses. Two notable sites along the route are the old Liebig House and the ruins of the Von Francois Fort. The former was once the residence of the copper mine's top brass, while the latter was used as a "Tronckenposten"- a drying outpost for alcoholic German soldiers in the early 1900s. Through the countryside of about 319km, a trip along this road be about five-and-a-half hours but the truck and its passengers were traveling just too slow on that day. Sitting for such long hours in the car Ishtar decided that it was excruciating to travel at such speed. Immediately she had an urge to escape. Her instincts suggested that she was about to reach her destination, not the one planned by the kidnappers but one pre-destined for her purpose. An inner voice directed her and explained what she had to do.

She was to move on foot with only her backpack. She didn't ask questions. As it was, Ishtar was getting tired of all the uncertainties. Today's quest she decided would be a leap of faith. Her spirit guide explained that she needed to head to the coast. The truth of her mission and understanding of self was to be revealed there. Ishtar trusts the universe enough to adhere to its call. Never did it lack in providing for her during her formative years. When she had no food, cloth or shelter, it provided and she contended. She lived happily and never question fade but that changed when she met Ben. The truth in him was overwhelming. It confused her, such that she feared him. His penetrating stare seemed to capture the deep insecurities she harbored and hid from the world. Just one stare felt as if he could tear out her heart and reveal her innermost secrets. Yet he never exposed it through utterances. He would simply point to the next action, which her heart executed without objection. Ishtar stayed by his side like a devotee. Following every walk and mimicking his actions. She was always enticed by intelligence and Ben ousted with more than natural. Without her asking, he would answer most accurately questions in her thoughts. Was he perhaps a magician or psychic she thought at times. Or simply knew her better than anyone she encountered during her quest. He was brave but did not fight. Not once. They met in Windhoek. Under the bridge where she was living with many others that dwelled in the streets. Survival on the streets of the capital involved constant fights, excessive use of substances and lack of sleep. You had to grow a heart of stone to be able to withstand all the challenges that came with it. She joined the streets by following her instincts, as she was used to the directing winds moving her body from one place to the next. Just like now, where she finds herself alone in the middle of no-where. With no guide and no clear plan. Ben came to her one night after she returned from the daily hustle. Found her in her little corner, preparing food in a big pot. He simply made himself home next to her and point to the pot. "Feeding the hungry and destitute, I see." he said. She looked at him and smiled in agreement. He sat there watching her silently. When she was done, she gave him some and they eat in silence. After that, she took the pot and placed it a few meters away from them. She turned back to him and waited but he just thanked her and moved back to his own corner. Ishtar cleaned their dishes and packed them away in her backpack and went to a mattress in the corner in preparations for the night. Later that night the others returned. The young ones ran directly to the pot and served themselves. It was an honored code. Everyone cared for the younger children. They fed and cloth them in unison. No one was to harm them. For the adults the code was different. Life was hard out there and the hustle real. You had to work for your own keep. Ishtar shared whatever she got from washing cars in the nearby park with the little kids. They in returned became her bodyguards. Because of their all-seeing eyes, nobody robbed her or meddled with her. For many were the instances that women were raped, robbed and mistreated on the streets such that it became second nature to them. But everyone stayed clear from Ishtar. Firstly because some believed that light emanated from and around her at night when she slept and secondly her new protectors slept in a circle around her. She worked for six days, from 9 am to 10 pm. I had an arrangement with the local park manager to use water and equipment for a minimal fee. Thus they could make use of the park's facilities at all times. This also created opportunities for her and the kids to bath in the park's public toilets before going back to the bridge. There were five of them and with stern discipline, she managed to get them off drugs and work with her to wash cars. They were safe in the park and played till late, only to return when they knew food was ready. It was a constant battle to fight the men that came by night looking for the kids. They would drive by the bridge slowly and flicker their lights. Like shadows, the kids would appear from everywhere and run to the cars. It was quick business and they acted swiftly. Some would drop off parcels to be sold while others would use the kids for their carnal pleasures. The next morning fights would erupt because money and drugs would have been stolen. The drug lords were hard on the kids and time and again young souls were eliminated when the kids could not cash in on time. The sex fanatics didn't make it easy for the street dwellers too. They practiced their hidden and hardcore fantasies on the small kids and sometimes didn't bother to pay them. Sexually transmitted diseases lived like a living soul amongst them as the night visitors refused protection. Ishtar was shocked by the harsh realities she observed on the streets. More so when she discovered that the monsters by night were the celebrities, business people, politicians, preachers, teachers, health workers and family men by day. The very same men whose cars they would clean by day. Men with straight serious faces pretending never to have met any of the street dwellers. She then understood why she was dropped into that environment. Growing up in foster care, she was told to value life and adhere to the principles of the world. One particular foster mother took time out to teach her wisdoms without focusing on ecclesiastical orientation but chose to teach her about spirituality. Ishtar was intrigued by anything metaphysical as it related with her soul thus she didn't need to study them through books. Thus in a way she was prepared because when the ugly of life stepped in, she learned not to question it but simply glide along the path fade laid for her. The first impulse was to reject the environment but the wise counsel of her foster mother was always with her. She could hear her loudly. "Never tag in objection to what life throws your way. Instead, receive it, analyze it, then see how it fits in the present, and make use of it. Never, ever, will the universe allow itself to send mistaken experiences to you? You get what is needed at that appointed time for the purpose needed then." With those words, Ishtar sat up and accept the new. Of course, she had to learn to fight off thugs and run from some but her guiding angle was never far or asleep. She knew and understand that this was a temporary exposure.

Days became months and she learned to beg on the streets. Once she even joined the kids to serve the night visitors. Her client was an old ugly, mean fat bully looking for a punching bag in the name of submissive sex fantasy. She gave him back in equal measure. Biting, scratching and beating. With a sore body and N $150.00 in the pocket, she sat out the next morning to observe the city life. Walking from one side of town to the other, until she found a beautiful little park in the middle of the city center. She went in there to rest her tired feed and soon fell asleep on the lovely lawn. While resting, she observed the many cars parked all around the park. Notice how people will park their cars and disappear for a long time. She could also see that many of this cars were dirty and her eyes opened to an opportunity of washing cars. The N$ 150.00 came in handy and she vowed never to serve a night visitor again. Until Ben came, things were seemingly better. She was on the streets for almost a year and resigned to her fade. He came and talk enlightenment to her weary heart. She listened and slowly realized that her mission has not yet unfolded.

At a very tender age she stopped wondering about her parents and family. She exchanged the thought of rejection with that of owning the world. Her parents and siblings would be the ones surrounding her sphere at the given time in life. Ben has thus filled the father figure and she listens to him diligently. Without fear, she did everything he asked her to do. One day he brought back a social worker and they enlisted the five kids in her care. It was a terrible day when they had to be transported to the government shelter. Ishtar felt like a mother whose children were forcibly removed from her. They all cried but understood that better opportunities awaited them at the shelter. The following month Ishtar walked each night to the shelter in Eros one of the lavish suburbs in the capital city to visit the children and return late to the bridge. The walking distance exhausted her and it strained her business. With the kids gone, she franchised the business to her neighbors. It turned into a violent noisy affair and the park manager put them all out. When she returned one night, frustrated and ready to give up. Ben smiled mysteriously and give her a number to call. The next morning he was gone and never returned. The shelter refused her access to the kids, as it interfered with their rehabilitation process and she was once again alone on the streets. She remembered a song that the wise foster mother use to sing and started singing it, "You lead I follow" somehow the song always managed to calm her spirit.

With a newsprint in her feet, she walked tall, back home. Before she reached the bridge she passed by a phone booth and placed a call to the number Ben gave her. Immediately the voice answered on the other side started talking. "Did you get the number from Ben he asked. " Yes, he said you would offer me a job, is that true? She inquired again. He answered affirmative and was didn't sound friendly either. Hurriedly he asked for her address and place the phone after she explained where he could find her. She waited but he never came until she was kidnapped that night. They were about 10 girls in the car and it was obvious that the guys were going to sell them. She trusted Ben. He seemed nicely put together and that assurance made her to trust him. They traveled at a very slow pace and soon the truck experienced mechanical problems on the dusty road. It was decided that they camp for the rest of the day and night while the men attend to the car and drive further the next day. That night the inner voice returned with urgency and she made a quiet escape. She ran straight to the dunes thinking that would be the best hiding place. But finally standing in front of a huge sand dune she realized that there was no easy way to get to the other side. She has to climb over. Slowly she attempts the first steps. However, every time she steps a second level up, her feet slip back to the beginning. Ishtar puts more effort but keeps falling back. Two steps to the front, slide back five steps. Therefore, it goes for some time and after a while, she gave up on walking and crawled all the way up to the top. Falling and crawling she came to the top and she let go and roll all the way to the floor bed. When she stood up there were more dunes in front of her. Ishtar walked for a few miles and then overcame with exhaustion plunged onto the sand. All her eyes could see was an unending sea of sand. Hopelessness caught up with her yet she refused to ask the daring question in her mind. It was not yet time she knew, and she didn't want to answer herself. This time she wanted to sit in front of a trusted being to ask questions. The cause of her life as it seemed now needed confirmation from another bigger source. She simply gave up to walk any further and made herself comfortable and slept right there on the sand.

Ishtar connected with other thoughts easily by way of dreams. Her guidance has always come through more clearly when her mind transports itself into unconsciousness. That night she found herself digging a hole in the desert. Strength from unseen forces was given unto her and she worked swiftly. The hole became bigger and clear water stared in her face. With a sudden rush, it pulled her in. She drifted in the water for a while, until realization dawned on her that, she was actually busy drowning in real life. Quickly she started paddling to the top but the waves pulled her down deeper. The little swimming exposure she had could not hold against the power of the tide. The waves circled around her to cause a spiraling effect. Down and down her body went into the deep. The long walk plus the struggle in the waters became unbearable and cased her memory to close in darkness. As her body was transported, the darkness started to fade. There was no more water and she drifted softly through the air until she landed on soft grass. Ishtar's body lay for long hours on the grass. While asleep, it was transforming itself. Her complexion deepening and the body defects healed, all the evidence of hardship experienced in the streets disappeared. When she finally woke up, her own, eyes could not see but she turned into a radiant beauty with flawless skin and perfect body. She felt rejuvenated and her bones were much stronger. On impulse, she started running. Starting slow and accelerating as she was getting used to the new body strength. Never did she knew she could run that fast. Her heart was beating well and her lungs staying in tune. For some reason, she could feel all the activity in her body, as if observing another being. She could track the activities of every vessel and body part. It was an amazing feeling. One experience Ishtar knew, without doubt, was part of her godly identity. For some time now, she knew that she was different from the normal children with whom she grew up. Her intellect and reason were matured and developed. She had no formal education but knew the ancient history of the earthlings, understood their political systems, governing bodies and religious practices better than others of her age. Her spirit guide told her as a young one how to use her mind to solicit information. Yet the fear of scorn and rejection had her hide under unfortunate environments. As she runs through the unknown space now. She knew that her discovery of self and the purpose of her existence would be revealed here. She didn't know where here was but it didn't matter. In the distance, her eye meets the changing nature. The perfect open space with only grass was ending. Lofty trees, tall and green. A variety of flowers and animals were in front of her eye. They all seemed peaceful. She ran closer and walk into that part of nature with silent awe. Transfixed to the majestic beauty unfolding before her. The animals were in unison. No one a prey to the other but all co-habiting in peace. Was this Heaven she wondered? It couldn't be, she reasoned for the world conditioned them that Heaven was above. She then remembered falling into a waterhole. Could it be that evil was playing tricks to her eye? How would she know? Who would tell her? Eagerly she started searching for a living being other than animals. Someone or something she could relate to. Looking behind every tree, bush and tall grass she moved deeper into the forest. There was no reason to be scared, all animals looked on her peacefully and the sounds surrounding was serene. At last, she came to a rock formation and approach it with caution. As she got close up the rocks parted and she entered. Every single action of Ishtar was in reaction to an impulse that urges her on spontaneously. She went through the opening without any fear. For Ishtar understood that the presence of her guiding angel was never absent. Every step she took into the unknown was done with confidence. As she has learned to trust his protective maneuvering of her walk. Deep within she knew that every single experience was pre-destined and she had to find the complete knowledge to submit to divinity. The change in her life's journey was constant. Never the same and always revealing a different level of manifestation. Her inner voice whispered that one day, everything would be made clear. The here and now was all she needed to act upon. The celestial experiences were not yet to be questioned.

From the beautiful scenery of nature, the cafe opened up a different life. The serenity was replaced by a bustling city life. She stood in front of a modern state in the heart of what looked like Alkebulan, but a much better version of it. People of color were busy with their daily chores. Mothers tending to their young while shouting gossip to their neighbors. Men rushing off to their different occupations. The buildings were tall and build with various precious stones. Her eye could see far and she identified different elements that made out the city. Right at her feet were the outskirts of the simpler lifestyles. Further, she saw an unfoldment of modern city life. Unlike the city she came from, this one was clean and organized. There were no street hawkers, every house was tended to perfection. There were little vegetable gardens behind each house. Though it seemed extremely developed, there were no cars and the presence of pollution in the air. The entire city was out of this world. Ishtar liked what she saw because her dream was unfolding right in front of her eyes. She always imagined perfect peace in the form that she was looking at now. Her heart felt at home. Then she looked further north into the distance. There was a tree with pink leaves flowing lovely in the soft breeze. It seemed as if light was emanating from the tree and moving in a circling formation. The light was slowly enclosing the entire city. It was like a life-giving or energy force. Her eye fixed on it and she started walking. Drawn by the light to investigate. To touch and smell or simply to sit underneath its presence. All of a sudden, a hand held her back. When she turned around a little boy was next to her.

"I'm sent to receive you to our house aunty." He said

"Where then is your house?" she smiled down at him.

He simply turned and point to a western direction. Away from the tree. Though there was a curiosity pulling her towards the tree, Ishtar held his hand and allowed him to lead the way through the city. They were walking, but she realized that everything moved swiftly passed them. As if they were flying or riding on an unseen vehicle. They reach the house within seconds and she was received by an elderly woman. Without a word she was offered both, food and clean sets of clothes. Whenever her eyes locked with that of the old woman the other just shook her head and left her alone. She was sent off to a beautiful room for the night. At the bedroom door, the old woman wish her a goodnight's rest with the promise. "The light will bring answers child."

The morning light opened up with the sounds of drums followed by a beautiful female voice. The song likened by a mystic morning bird filled the air surrounding the city. Yesterday's beehive of activities turned into a new musical experience. Everyone dressed in traditional attire emerges singing from houses. All moving towards the rock opening through which Ishtar entered the city. The voice of the lead singer was clear as day and heard beyond the city, above all other voices.

"We come together with our fathers and mothers,

See your children approaching in one voice to sing a song of gratitude,

A song of worship to you our ancestors,

Giving tithes and offerings to the one true God,

Pray to him to accept our offerings today,

We come to you as one,

Children of the soil,

Children of the sun,

See your time has just begun,

Search before your eyes,

To see the City of Gold in all its glory,

Come children come,

Bring your offerings before the Lord,

Today may mark the beginning of a new day,

The womb man to lead the quest of discovering,

The New City of Gold has arrived,

Come my people come,

Let us sing and dance for the Lord,

With good cheer,

We bid you morning our mothers, our fathers, our children

And our companions on this space called Kumta,

Known to the world outside as Area-51

The mighty city between the two worlds,

The guiding fire has been burning for the last two weeks,

Eagerly we have been waiting for the day that understanding of the two worlds would be made one,

Come to my people,

Come all,

To the animal kingdom to lend but one voice to the Creator,

To offer our tidings and stand at the altar as one servant,

Seeking the face from the most divine,

Moro, Moro, we come together with our ancestors,

Our mothers, our fathers,

Hear the song of your children and behold the new day,

I hope we stand."

The music soon reached a climax and people started dancing wild, some chanting and others screaming wild. It was an organized noise. People kept in tune with the musical instruments and only increased tempo at the climax of its sounds. The song was repeated until the lead singer was certain that everyone was gathered in the open plains of the animal kingdom.

Woken by her host Ishtar was also among the people, with the little boy (the guide) next to her. She did not know any of the people around her and an unsettling energy rise within her. It was the first time she was in a place where her heart was silent and not able to guide her. She was accustomed to moving between different places and lifestyles but always knew what was expected of her to do. Today is indeed the first that she stands in the unknown, watching what others are doing. Her guiding spirit has disappeared and there was complete silence in her heart. Then she notices that she was dressed in a white gown. Hers being the only mono tune dress while everyone else was dressed in colorful outfits. Every face that her eye met gave her a gentle welcoming smile and their eyes were shining full of love. Ishtar felt welcome and her mind began to settle in peace. Her inner being remaining silent. She stood there, cloth beautifully. Yet experience nakedness because her inner being has left her.   Then she wondered if this was how death felt. Was she alone now? Which part of her being was representing her now? Was it the spirit body or the physical? If she was dead? It could not be the physical but why then was her heart silent. Why then was the voice within silent. She was still pondering with the thoughts when the little boy touched on her sleeve.

"Yes dear, what is wrong?" she asked

He looked at her with concerned and then giggled.

"You do not know really do you?" he asked.

"Know what?"

"Stop talking to yourself so loudly." He said, pointing his little fingers to the crowd in front of her. "Everyone can hear you. You are distracting them."

"What do you mean? I was just thinking. Did I speak out loud?"

"No aunty, here you only have one voice. What you say by mouth and what you do not say. We can hear all that."

"How is that possible? How can they hear me think?"

"I do not know aunty. We always hear. I could hear more as a baby until I learn to speak. Now I hear both the tongue and mind clearly. Sometimes it is confusing and that is why I stay with the Oracle."

"You mean to tell me that everyone in this city can hear my thoughts?"

"Yes. Don't they do that where you are coming from?"

"No, they surely don't."

"But why? Are they not like us?"

"That is what I need to know as well, child. You said you are staying with the Oracle. What is that? Don't you stay with your grandmother?"

"My grandmother is the oracle. Where are you from? It seems you do not know much?"

"Yes seems I really do not know much."

"But where are you from then. My granny told me not to ask you anything but now everyone is wondering."

"Are they? They are not even looking at us."

"So you can't hear also? Can you not hear them asking each other?

"Ahaaaaa.....no I cannot."

"Really? Just listen more...do not think of anything else just listen."

Ishtar stood silently for a while then said. "I can only here a bustling noise, like a sound of running water."

From behind the old woman answered.

"That is good enough for now. All babies start to hear that sound before any other thing. That is the sound of separation child, you are at the right place. Come with me." She said while looking down gently at the boy. "As for you dear one, hush. Did I not ask for total silence? You were not to ask her anything."

Ishtar step in between to help the boy. "Please do not be angry, he was just innocent and being a child."

The old woman laughed. "We never get angry here child. That is an unpleasant gift for the other world. He is not a child either, he is 84 years older than you are. Please walk with me."

"He...but...he said you are his grandmother?"

"Indeed I am. His parents were exiled and I had to take him in."

"Why were they exiled?"

"They fled from their purpose of creation. Come, dear, let us begin with the ceremony. All questions will be answered in due course."

With that, the Oracle started singing the same morning song. Ishtar looked at her with wonder. She did not think for a moment that the old woman would be the lead singer. While the song proceeds, the Oracle looked at her and smile. "Do not worry I have two voices, I send the singing voice out early to wake others for the ceremony while I was preparing myself." When Ishtar opened her mouth to ask. She placed a finger on her lips and joined her voice in song. The people followed her all the way to the throne of the Lion King. The Oracle was the only one that bowed before the King. Both animals and humans were equal in this world hence none superior in thought, power, and purpose. Thus, the Oracle's bowing was not to the animal kingdom but instead to the greater being within him.

"I greet you great and dear friend of our people. Your daughter is here again to adorn your paradise with splendor and joyful noise. Allow us entry to the gates of the Highest. The time to present the Daughter of the Four Winds has finally come."

"Dear one form the Great Divine. Upon you, always remains the blessings of our fathers and of the Lord. I am but a servant but the supreme to serve you and your great nation. Never will the gates to the heavens be shut for you dear Queen of the people."

"I thank you for your grace dearest friend and guardian of our joint worlds. May favor always remain with you and within the plains."

"And to you the ever able presence that is never the absence, I bid you."

With those words, the Lion roared and the sky above thundered. Lighting strike and the earth trembled. When the second roar was heard both animal and human bow to the ground. The heavens parted and light like a staircase beamed to the surface of the plain. The Oracle held out the hand of Ishtar and lead her into the light. They stood there until the thunder stopped. Instead of the expected thunderous rains, a light breeze of rain fell to the grounds. Everyone shout of joy and celebrations started in full swing. All of a sudden, there was more dancing and music. With Ishtar in her hand, the Oracle climb to the throne of the Lion King and present her to the people and animals. The Lion roared the third and final time and spoke to those before him.

"For centuries upon end, we offered the sweet-sounding sacrifice to the gods. Time after time it was rejected. Some of our own children objected later and left our world to join the earthlings and other species in different parts of the universe. They became bitter and spread lies and anger in the world, thus silencing the voices of truth, rubbishing them to nothing. They started eating the flesh of each other and polluted the once pleasant sight of the earth. Indeed the fulfillment of the prophecy had come to be. For it was good for the patient at heart and the faithful believer to witness the promise coming to life. After 1000 years the gods have finally received our daughter amongst the chosen citizens of the cosmos beyond us. Through her will be revealed the awaited knowledge of the truth. Her presence will ignite the compasses pointing to the golden trail and reactivate the hidden wonder. The lost glory and hope of the people will be restored. Through millennia, the earthlings were enslaved, tortured and raped for their wisdom, power, and prestige. Caught up by deception and simple pleasures of the world, they betrayed each other and sold their inheritance to the fairer of skin. Today marks the beginning of an exodus for our people. Guided by the fierce Ishtar, behold the revolutions of Great Alkebulan begins. We will repossessed, concur and restore Alkebulan. Let us celebrate today and tomorrow. Soon Ishtar will birth a new promise of hope to her people." With loud cheers, the people came one by one to hug Ishtar, the animals bow before her and they proceed dancing and feasting on delicacies of the field.

The only person not able to celebrate was Ishtar. For she did not understand what was happening and above all too afraid to ask or even think. She sat quietly on the lush green grass and looked at the dancing crowd. The boy came to her with a full plate of exotic fruits and present them to her.

"Here, eat and fill your body. It will give you energy because we are going to dance and celebrate for two days." With that and childlike energy, he jumped to his feet and runs to join the dancing party. The Oracle joined her where she was sitting and gently stroke her hands.

"Never mind, child. As promised, I will explain everything to you after the celebrations. We cannot break the code earlier than that else the seal will not unlock itself. Be glad, be merry. The skies favor you, thus no harm will ever come to you. Now eat well and join the others they want to know and speak to you. Allow them, they mean only good."

The place where Ishtar found herself was called Area-51. Scientist in the earthly realm discovered it but made it out as a new alien base as they could not enter it. Oracle Mable moved her people to that space from the Land of Punt when

Memnon desecrated the holy land, during the ancient times. It remained hidden for years until the civilized order started meddling in the affairs of the universe. The oracle knew that they could not remain hidden for long and was glad that Ishtar was ordained that day by the gods to take up her mantel and start working. On the third day she explained just briefly to Ishtar how everything fell into place, the rest she had to experience on own accord.

CHAPTER FIVE

After the encounter with Oracle Mable and the citizens of Area -51, Ishtar returned back to the upper world mysteriously. She had to observe the political changes of the world from a distance before she could provide support. From the worlds of the gods there was no division. Every men was equal as he was a perfect representation of the creator. If ever there would be something in the realm of the gods that confused their minds, was the spirit of separation which bred in the hearts of the earthlings. For this phenomena to be investigated and understood on all levels of existence, Ishtar had to endure the experiences she had. Though the earthlings were progressive and many different races met and intermarry on global front. There existed a deep underlining hatred towards each other. Ishtar surveyed her territory and decided that it was wise to start within the holds of the modern day history. The ancient history was clear but what followed during and after the lighter skinned people invaded Alkebulan was to be investigated. Empowered by her ordination at Area 51 she was able to use her celestial powers. Though she needed to learn how to merge the body and spirit as one, she knew it wouldn't hurt to use her third eye to scan the surface of the world. Her ear was constantly irritated by the word racism, which was a system of cultural, institutional, and personal values, beliefs, and actions in which individuals or groups were put at a disadvantage based on ethnic or racial characteristics they portray. Instantly Ishtar knew that the foreigners with fairer skin were the engineers of this system. They were the ones putting up processes of division be it knowingly or unknowingly because the master mind behind it all was Memnon. Those that executed his plans thought it was for the greater purpose of the light skinned but unfortunately Memnon had his own plans. However, the system worked because over a span of 400 years or more steadfast and systematic discriminatory maltreatment of the black race was at the order of the day. Alkebulanians were denied the most fundamental and inalienable of all human rights. There was a widespread and common belief that Alkebulanians on homeland and diaspora were enjoying democracy and freedom in a post-colonial ear. However, the fairer skinned had no such intentions, how could they. They build the infrastructures of Alkebulan and other continents they conquered for their personal advancement. Introduced western education and lifestyles for their comfort. When the colonized screamed foul play they recognized their value in terms of skilled labour and trained them accordingly. The purpose of such training was to introduce a culture, language, religion, values and knowledge of their supposedly superior conqueror. Unfortunately the manipulated Alkebulanian bought into it all. Now sitting in the Namibian space Ishtar acknowledge that there was much to do. As it looked, forgiveness was not a topic to introduce without teaching them how to believe in themselves and stand with pride in their own identity as a people. Only a person that knows his worth, power and love can and will forgive another his error. She humbled herself to the understanding that Amma was wise and choose the right being and place to serve the purpose.

Thus, for Ishtar's work to commence in full, Namibia was the perfect country to carry out the search for answers. With its young independence they still had memories fresh enough from the apartheid regimes and of the liberation struggle. A small country thus torn between its mandate of reconciliation and cameradie towards those that aid its struggle to freedom. The leadership understood the importance of keeping peace. Not only within their tribes but also with the locally born foreigners who engineered the economic soundness of the country. It was thus not that simple to throw out the old to introduce the new. For the new thoughts could not exists without the foundations laid down by the old. Though its independence was a majority win, there were underlining things the eye could not see. Beneath the layer of victory by the black race was hidden the truth of the money lender who brought the guns and medicine into the exiled camps of the liberation warriors. The same powers that supported the colonial rulers who sought to represent from within the country's walls. The supporters provided not only guns and medicine. They sponsored education in foreign countries. Under the blanket of various ideologies the small nation of Namibia and its leaders were brainwashed into succumbing to the teachings of those with a hidden agenda. As Alkebulan was sold out thousands of years ago to the very same foreigner that came through pretense to help the son of the soil to gain independence from the oppressor. He needed to adhere to the demands of the one holding the wallet. So it came that the sons of the soil sold their ancestral blood stained independence back into the hands of the one that owned them already. Disguise as a friend, they introduced world money lending schemes that robed the states of Alkebulan from true independence. Yet again, the sons of the soil rushed into another trap and betrayed the Motherland. Memnon's offspring thus had a perfect plan in place to remain rulers of the world. With unseen hands they re-wrote history. Change religion into their gain and design systems that would cripple Alkebulan for the gain of others. They were skillful in setting their master plan in motion. See, before the liberation struggle and subsequent freedom. The people of the land were conditioned by missionaries into a religion far removed from their practices. They were conditioned into believing that who they were and how they lived as a people was barbaric and not acceptable in the modern world. Just like in the ancient days where the wise were prosecuted in the name of change. The Alkebulan house was broken down from the root. The track in the field to the holiest places of worship to the gods and ancestors was burned down. They were given books with a foreign tongue to read. Required to learn to speak in foreign languages, eat foreign foods and pray to one foreign god only. It was difficult for the son of the soil to discern the truth which was written in the book of the missionaries. It had reflections of their past but in the names of others and of unknown places. Yet they could identify with some of its history, for it was not theirs. There was no other history. They were the first and they were the only source that walked with the creators on the soil and heard their voices directly. But with the key to the House of Truth in the hands of the foreign child they couldn't proof anything. One major thing that foreigner knew was the power of the women. Hence, they lured them into submission with kindness. Let them to their bedchambers and forced them into bearing sons and daughters with mixed blood.   For they understood the power of love a mother has for her offspring. They messed up her mind. Brainwashed her with new ideologies and robbed her from sanity. As she was contaminated it would take years upon a hundred to cleanse her royal bloodline. And these the foreigner knew, hence his plan to capture her and distort the future generation. With her heart split in two they knew, she would rise men to respect their fathers and obey to the loving and forgiving heart of the mother. As a men never detaches from the apron, he abide to all that he was taught at the breast. How then could the Alkebulan men stand tall in a world contaminated by blood? Deep rooted and successful was the plan of the greedy few. Clutching Alkebulan under chains of helplessness. As the world was ruled by money they soon lend from the west and when they revolt against the moneylender's conditions. Access to money would be stopped with trading sanctions imposed. The blood flowing through the veins of the sons of the soil was stubborn and he would keep rebelling. His stubbornness plunging the struggling land into more oppression. No longer could they eat and drink. No longer harvest their own and mine their wealth. For they were taught that knowledge as could only be obtained from the moneylenders was power. Their hands were not functioning anymore. They needed and believe that by reading the books of others they could create wealth. Under such chaos was born the independence of a small country to which Ishtar was posted. Since her reincarnation, thirty years ago they struggled between insanity to keep their little world perfect. They had leaders with pure hearts and leaders blinded by Memnon's manifesto. Those that believed that to steal from its own was the only way out of poverty and those that tried to reconcile their own and others. In their quest to maintain peace they rushed through collaborations with both west and east. In this process burying themselves more in debt and selling the only remaining pieces of worth to the highest bidder. The country was crumpling. People started ethnicity war amongst each other. The government was on its knees as those trusted with the country's funds stole it and covered themselves with gold. The once majestic country which has become the hope of the Motherland as its base of reformation was in ruins. The new moneylender showed his face and made his conditions known. The country belonged to him now. For the sons of the soil could not repay their loans. Thus, the lender started off by closing all harbours, airports and mines of the people. He understood by capturing their money generators he would have total control. He didn't need the disguise he was operating under anymore. Over the years he became good friends with the leaders. Spraying them with gifts in brown envelopes and assisting them in everything the west was withholding from them. His strategies worked and while the sons were playing with the new toys. The lender build his masterful plan all around the borders of Alkebulan. The lender had many offspring breed in incubators to flood the continent of Alkebulan. Within a short span of time they infiltrated and cunningly overtook the leaders' houses. By the time the gifts run out and the toys became boring there was no home to call to.

On this day that water was becoming scares and fear of survival made itself known in the mind of the sons. They remembered that their forgotten ancestors left a trail for them to follow. A trail which was to re-invent the wheel and set them free for good. They were not alone for Memnon knew that secret as well and has been observing the forces at play with a keen eye. As the sons raised up to return to the bosom of their mothers. So did the others as well by pressing buttons to release the warriors to guard them off. Ishtar could sense all that and needed a place to strategize and set her plan in motion.

The heart of man was the same no matter how he chose to live. Though the mind was conditioned to the extremes. One could never penetrate beyond the permission granted by its owner. This one entity was the biggest hurdle for Memnon. As much as he trained, initiated and conditioned somehow his subjects found a way to disobey him. As soon as they tasted power they would try to derail his plan in an effort to take over his glory. Under the blankets of a new dynasty wars were fought to take over the leading position. Greed was once again showing its face in the underworld of those who wished to rule the world. Each governor on the continent tried to outsmart the other. They build machinery and breed deceases to destroy each other. They signed bi-lateral agreements and allies while spying and plotting against each other. While fighting their respective worlds they all understood the hidden powers of Alkebulan and tried to either damage or safe it. For the first time Memnon was in doubt. His great plan was growing out of bounds and overtaking him. He was losing control and feared that his great deception was going to turn into his destruction. As fear crept into his heart. Memnon became weak and sloppy. His subjects got the upper hand and killed him. As each continent's governor was plotting to destroy him it was difficult for one to claim victory of his demise. With

Memnon's fall, each continent was free to rule itself once more. Carrying some of the mandate as laid down by Memnon. He died at the age of 150. A spirit which has not completed its purpose on earth never enters the gates of the afterlife. It roams around looking for a new body temple to use, such that his mission can be accomplished. Memnon was such a spirit. He re-incarnated immediately. This time born and raised in the same house of the governor of the great Kingdom of America. Today standing in the able body of its presidency. Memnon executes his plan of world dominion perfectly. Rebuilding the Americas into a great nation again.

Unfortunately they were not alone. His total focus was to make the west great, forgetting that he had played the same card of deceit in the south and east of the world. While the fathers were playing chess. From the House of Commons raised a mighty daughter. They thought she was perfect as the gate keeper of their transportation and device against the sources they were deceiving. She was the bridge that the great new church and the League of Nations needed to execute their plans favourably. But she was female. Born with the heart of nurturing and care. While they ponder, create and destroy she swam through the undercurrents of change. Well, she was female and beautiful. Memnon and his subjects desired to own her bedchambers. Guile, hiding behind innocence she flirt with them while creating her own master plan. They had the wealth, they had the people's minds and they had the secrets. She lived on a deserted island, trespass at will by the mighty with her only strength her beauty. Not only did she observed the one far afield but she took greater interest in the one hidden in her bosom, the Knight of Mighty 12. Hidden in her own fields to guard the secrets what would make others create. What her face tantalized, her waist called out and her swing boosted. The Knights knew no woman before and she soon served the sweat wine and bread. Luring them into trust and isolating them in lust. No, she never bedded any, but she knew what a man in lust would do for a woman. The brought her flowers and cloth her. Soon she greeted them into speaking of the hidden secrets. Slowly she raised with the knowledge of Memnon's vision. She saw through his plan and also figured out the lack of success thereof. He was grooming men and men were fiddle minded. They had the same take on everything. They read, they saw and they act. None of them looked deeper than the obvious. None seek to understand why one would overpower them each and every time. They were promised gold and continue seeking gold everywhere. She came slowly of age. Deciding to harvest more than just gold and fine linen. But for her to do that, she needed a ruling chair. While the governors of the other continents looked elsewhere. Fixing their eye on strategies to overcome Memnon. She build weapons of destruction by night under the disguise of a modern garden to feet warriors. Her harvest would be distributed throughout the continents in support of those at war. Yet within the sources send out was poison. Her garden of fruit and vegetables was no longer only to feed the House of Commons. She introduced the importance of simple things to hook them to her food. Carrots which was in affluence she made known as the source behind winning wars at night for men could see well if they eat then. She baked and served them shepherd's pie which was advertised as the best to accompany a shepherd during his service. Within the food she exported was hidden poison made from the same plants she harvest that killed the ruling warriors and their leaders. They could not blame her for any death and that which could not be proven made her powerful. Soon she ascended the throne and build a commonwealth under the disguise of care. She was great and ruled over those assigned to her on other continents. She was the only royal amidst dignitaries without blue blood. Their gold, diamonds, iron and animals. All were registered under her name. She mined them and send them overseas, recreate them into other consumables and sold them back to the original owners. But she was friendly and shared her food and education with them. Soon they spoke her language better than her own sons and daughters and they built her island into the Great United Kingdom it became. Her sons were not happy and loot and spoiled the plans she carefully crafted. With fury she sent them to a prison built in the distant south. For the island was not equip to house the overflow of wrong doers. This sons born of a cunny mother knew the best strategies of warfare. Silently and with simple approached they built an equal fortress for themselves with the same skills used by their mother. However, they too had difficulty of cutting the umbilical cord. Thus remain dutiful to serve the Commonwealth. Wealth of Alkebulan that was shared equally to all except those in Alkebulan. This was Memnon's world and as confusing as it seemed, all over his plan was stressing out of bounds. Even the little yellow tribe far in the east, smell the rat and started working on mightier weapons and theories to overtake and overpower those that has identified themselves as the mighty powers. Only Alkebulan remained dormant in the holds of masters ruling all over her. Wailing at the sight of her defeat. Memnon's plan was confined in many conspiracy theories but the plan was equally confusing his greater vision. This made him laugh with satisfaction. For Memnon knew that no matter what the outcome no female was going to regain power and he had the ultimate secret to overpower any governor that succeed to overtake the new world. The only thing lacking was the map to the trail. Once he has that in his hands the puzzle would be complete.

Missions were overwhelming but Ishtar knew that she had to get through them all one by one. Her next stop was in a little town in the northern parts of Namibia.

Where the sycamore trees and jacaranda sing songs of merry existence. The place where love was destined to meet life and procreate the beautiful elements of humanity needed to serenate this part of the world. From this little village was to come forth only beauty which was to be found amongst the race called human. Instead it was cloaked with the sting of lust and hatred. Yes, the maidens were extremely beautiful and the men divine in their appearance of the golden gift of the gods. They were specially created to assist in the procreation of humanity. This was the special antidote against all the previous experiments of giving life to creatures which became a scorn to the House of the Lords. In the other worlds some stood as giants representing the physic of angels but lack in the features of beauty, some were disfigured and hidden from the Motherland, living on Area-51 and revert to as aliens. Though all had the right to inherit the peace of the soil. The goddess of beauty and grace took it upon her to sow a seed of beauty in the heart of Tsumeb. A town so beautiful and its vegetation was intact for pro-creation. Alongside the seed of beauty existed the law of matrimony which was to perfect the previous principles of the sacred union. Men and women of this town were not destined to intermarriage but had to be release into the open fields of the world and find themselves mates from other tribes. They had the power to travel far and wide and built homes not just emanating beauty but longevity of spouses in marriage and change societal and cultural believes of man marrying many wives, thus breaking the principles of sound and happy living for its offspring. Through this new phenomena women were introduced back into society as the homemakers and disciplinarians of their children such that decency was reborn. However, this was only able at the length of life of the host. As soon as the first generation of women and men born under the original seed passed the gates of life into death. The underdogs took over. Soon the seed of beauty was scorned and celebrated in places which it was not meant to be. Pageants were held to compete against the other's beauty in return for money. The overall winner was idolized and both men and women soon join into the game disguised under the banner of world peace. Instead of reintroducing the traditional marriage with its fundamentals, people were exposed to various lifestyles choices. The rules changed, men had the final say of how and with whom they wished to marry. The first wives were no longer responsible to approve the next marriage, or decisions surrounding the proper management of the house. The children were no longer raise in union but in separation. With it was born the single parent and step parent syndrome, which was far removed from the ways of living of the people of Alkebulan. This new trend gave power to single parents making decisions in raising their offspring without the consent of the community or nation.

CHAPTER SIX

Alkebulan fell into the hands of the greatest deceit. There couldn't be a claim of demonic interference. Though everything started with Memnon's influence. The Alkebulanians had enough time to change the cause of events, yet they chose not to. Thus, they brought the great kingdom to its fall was its own fabrication through greed. Throughout times immemorial they sold out on self and didn't bother about the future of its own generations. The citizens were hyped up by a fierce competitive spirit which refused to build on a common achievement and instead, gathered its own riches for personal gain. They once chanted 'Ubuntu ama Bantu' phrase today turned into 'every men for himself and Amma for all'. Amma's creation was to be self-sufficient and filled with compassion to be its brother's keeper. This was not enough for the fallen men of Alkebulan. The new leading breed were born of mothers with an evil eye that were consumed with hearts that sought only after gold. The rush for gold that has in fact seen many killed as they trekked through unknown worlds, digging deep like scavenges into the soil, eating and living in dungeons they called mines. Just to own a golden stone which would have them eat well for only a couple of years and thrust them back into misery for the rest of their lifetime. They kept chasing after the gold.

No, the sons of Alkebulan became blind to the wisdom of their ancestors. They were living without a purpose and believing only the modern confusion which arrived from those leading their folk to extinction. In the current political houses were Alkebulanian leaders rule. The game was different. They all listened to the voice of Memnon and followed like marionettes. However, the seed of the warrior womb-men had planted some responsible and, free thinkers amongst the crowd. These sons of Alkebulan joined political forces in different states all around the continent. In Libya, they had one that was rich with gold and other minerals. He was leading his people without the social grants from Big Uncle Sam or Little Yo Sing. He proved to be the thorn in the flesh of those that equally built systems and laws that would ridicule a born free Alkebulanian. The great Libyan attended conferences travelling in the tradition of his ancestors. He carried his tents, his slaves, even his food and spoon; never to dine with the foreign lenders that pretend to rule the world as a puppet. His brothers were however weak and afraid to support his course. Today, they are sitting in mud and gutted by their own little images, looking into the sorry fat bellies they have manifested.

Another son like that was raised from the soil of Namibia. Soft spoken and dear to his people's heart as his main interest was to free education for his people and introduce new ways of learning which would not only benefit the people of the small country but open opportunities for them all across the globe. He started out late and was silence by life in the prime of his age. He was not like those who were taking after him and leading without any vision. He was not like them who were committing crimes of education so great to the future generation of the soil. He left them as beggars on the sides of the streets. Ishtar's eye that sees far identified these men and women who were trying vigorously to bring about change in Alkebulan. They all weren't leaders of political might but, there were great modern Gadhafis, Marcels, Kenyattas and Mandelas, the Bikos, Mugabes, !Gobs, Witboois and the Mahereros. Though the great names were assassinated because they wanted to change the lifestyles of their people and bring them back to glory, the modern ones were trying to step back into those great shoes of their forefathers. It's those unseen heroes to whom Ishtar's attention is directed; the woman that tends to her community gardens which feeds 500 people and the lady with the soup kitchen, who takes care of the elderly and orphans. It was also the man across the street making wooden prosthesis for war amputees, the artist that captures the beauty of Alkebulan's forest, animals and people in beautiful images and the nurse that volunteers in war zones. It was the doctors that serve without the limitation of borders, the engineer that declined the Harvard scholarship to teach the poor sons and daughters of the soil and the general cleaner that understands what submission means so that they can better educate their children and provide for a future. It was as well the Indian Herb smoker that sits amongst his kinsmen to add a word of wisdom which his people have forgotten. These are all true warriors who will change the times for Alkebulan; for the leader is corrupted to the core. Indeed, he won't relinquish his throne easily. Thus, the ultimate war won't be against Memnon, but Alkebulan against its own. Unfortunately, some would be illuminated so that a new reform can come into being. Again, blood may flow, some for the good of the continent while others would simply be murdered. It will be a sad victory but one that will bring Alkebulan back to life. Ishtar's heart is pained for there will come a time when she will stand alone against the children of Alkebulan as none of its mothers would agree to fight against their offspring. She would need to walk through that stream alone with only the support from the animal world. She would also need to invest trust in those that would walk on the gold trail and convince them that war was imminent but could be avoided. It won't be easy, for upon creation, Amma served all the offspring with celestial powers, which can't be repossessed. They will know how to war against the unseen and unknown. For the Sangoma has long surpassed the use of her talents for good health and tidings only. The all seeing eye of the gods has expanded the realm inviting evil incantations to feed the greedy souls of the children of Alkebulan. Thus, the war would be fought on levels and dimensions not only of the carnal but the spirits or gods as well. Some will succumb to their own unwise decisions; some will unfortunately succumb due to lack of knowledge. This is Alkebulan in present day. Where both leader and subject are caught up in a self-fabricated wind cluster of greed and the need of survival while lost to the advancement of the world outside their own jail. They provided the wool that spun the web that has captured them and allowed their carnal bodies to rule the spirit which was reincarnated within. The one to serve a divine living purpose. The duties of the eyes and ears was swopped and the taste buds of the mouth became its leader. Why then wouldn't the ancestor turn their backs on its own and giving them up to the open galaxies beyond to deal with them accordingly? Why then wouldn't the Mother Earth cry out in despair?

CHAPTER SEVEN

While other planets were created with lack, Planet C-53 was created to advance beyond all others. The Creator's eye was gentle on Planet C-53 and they thought that by giving them an image similar to theirs, earthlings would unleash great powers within them, unmatched by any other in the galaxy. They were meant to be the first love, and choice to the future of evolution. Unfortunately, from inception of the great idea, they chose not to conform to the mandate of the greater forces. They decided that they were the ultimate source of life and did as they pleased.

Now that she had understanding of the political and cultural ways of the people Ishtar took a closer look at the lifestyles unfolding in various homes and communities. This were supported to happen as she was growing up but the foster houses didn't offer her much insights into the lives of ordinary citizens. There was no need for Ishtar to engage in physical contact with the people. With the powers to her aid she could simply zoom into different homes, space and time. She liked being in control that way rather than to explain herself to people. And with that understanding her unfoldment began. Her experiences started to unfold in the heart of the country. She came out of nowhere and experienced every single thing which was happening all around her. She was classified as a woman, something she did not understand because her spirit was not defined by gender. In her previous life she was unique and greater than the name or gender, but on this part of the soil, they normalised her existence to that of a woman, an entity known as a mother, a wife, a daughter, a sister, a priestess, or even a witch. She became one and all of them. The way she is perceived depended on the position she occupied, and the different perceptions were reflected through songs, works of art, music, language, and religion. She represented the women tribe fully as she unfolded. Women, adorned with respect and splendor. Looked upon as she gracefully fashioned the world around her in perfection, a perfect picture of beauty, grace, and love. That was what her body temple represented before time and malice changed her position. Today the young brothers through song titled her a bitch. Equating her existence to that of a canine. A species lowest ranked in the animal kingdom planet. Domesticated it was, given partial love and accepted as a choice pet. This was the new version of women, far removed from the divine idea of glory and grace she was created for. However in some parts of the piece of soil they called home. Same level of value was given to a woman when she became a mother. Motherhood, therefore, the referred and precious position in new Africa. Becoming a mother lay emphasis on two main parts of a woman's body. The breast and the vaginal organ which was elaborated. They believe her womanhood had the power of life and death, while the breast fostered growth. Though given such low esteem, women still wanted to be wives. They got married, though in many communities and tribes they are seen as slaves or properties. Wives unlike mothers were valued only for the purpose of procreation and then cast aside. Woe, to the one that couldn't produce children, she was subjected to scorn and daily humiliation. Not only by men but also by her own female sisters. Thus forcing them to go to extreme lengths of getting a child, be it through a concubine, surrogate mother or at times through dubious means robbing another of her own. It became the ultimate desperate cry for women in her quest to remain married to obtain the sacred crown. The crown which listed her amongst the respected and titled. Knowing that would her name disappear with it. Before marriage, she was someone's daughter, someone's sister and just someone's something. By marriage, she became someone's wife and through giving birth she was someone's mother.

Her name and her natural worth never featured. She was just it. Not understanding the significance thereof they did it with so much grace and pride. The husband took the royal status of a king. His only role defined to rule over the weaker species, be it women, child or animal. This is the truth the new warrior learned from the masses around her but she knew it would be the women who were going to drive the mission with her. Though it didn't make any sense at all it was important to recognize that things were completely messed up on the motherland. The fairer skinned people had no regard for them thus it was entirely up to the Alkebulanian people to save themselves. With the understanding she was gaining, she was more willing to aid them and stand in the gab of times.

Westerners continued to pretend that the Alkebulanian people were savages. That they didn't know anything about civilization. And presented their own achievements as the best. The native people's only weakness was that they were bound by a culture to receive a stranger as long as he/she was friendly and peaceful. Thus many disguise themselves as friends while they plot and scheme on the continent. They asked questions of interest and received their answers from the natives. They tried things on themselves which would fail each time. With laughter in their eyes for the stupidity of the foreigner, Alkebulanians would reveal their secrets. The foreigners would fell sick and the natives will bring them back to life and gave them one that would never leave them again, a life closer to mortality. These fascinations crept into the hearts of the foreigners and they reconcile it with the agenda from their master. They realized that it was time to uncover more hidden secrets and keep it to themselves. Greed overtook them once again and with each new discovery they wanted ownership and killed those from whom they collected the truth. The easiest way to do was to create viruses to destroy the people and remove the knowledge which could safe them. By the time most people in Alkebulan realized that they were deceived it was far too late. They were completely emerged in the ways of the strangers. They ate as they did, practice worship as they did and also fixed their sacred health the way they did. The biggest commodity next to the distorted word of truth presented to them was medication for the body temple. Forgotten was the wisdom that the body temple was able to heal itself with herbs found in their fields. Fields which were soon destroyed to build schools, houses, hospitals, giant mines, even unknown plants that would kill them. In the eye of the new breed of Alkebulanians, that which they saw and taste was civilization. Not the rich, powerful and peace reigning past they had. They reduced themselves poor before the great new unknown and taught their children to respectfully follow in their steps. They listen to the voice of the foreigner who became their supporter during their revolutionary freedom fight. They listen to the voice that told them that everything with a lighter skin was better. They told them that their own lighter skinned brethren were fathered by the foreigner. Forgetting that thousands of years ago. Light skinned blue eyed offspring were birth by priestesses in the mountains of Alkebulan. Children that carried the mark of divinity and eyes that could see distant things. By lending out their ear, they killed and mutilated such beings. And overtime these very beings, tired of executions, built themselves sanctuaries in a different sphere. They covered their tracks very well and remain in isolation. Only the gods and those favoured by them could access that land. One of such was the land where Ishtar met with Oracle Mable for the first time. Where both animal and human commune in peace. Just as much as the deceivers were creating killer diseases and bringing them to the continent in disguise. Silently, those living in the unknown world kept healing their people. They did it discretely such that it kept the wondering eye of the scientist at bay. For the wise knew that every single thing stolen from the House of Bulan was available in parts all over the three visible worlds. The one at sea, the one on the ground and the one below the sea. Unfortunately, the strange healing and resistance was notice and interpreted wrong. Human trafficking increased, and body parts were sold on the black market. Unfortunately Ishtar was unable to help the girls she was kidnapped with during her escaped as it was not yet the appointed time to start her work and they also ended up as victims of the traffickers. These traffickers were selling people to certain cruise ship management as sex slaves or to black markets that harvest and sold human organs. During this time false prophets from Alkebulan also rose with greed written all over them. These were boys raised in good homes by caring mothers. Boys that read the book of the foreigner and prayed on it. Boys that devoted their time to the white church and not to Amma. Boys who learned everything from the masters in high temples. They saw the influence the word had on people. They became rich and influential and decide to follow in the steps of the influencers. Blessed as the offspring of Alkebulan, they knew where to find powers to increase their wisdom and thus sold themselves to the world. They once again deceived their own for a pot of gold.

Everyday news broke out on kidnappings of women and children. Of passion killings and body mutilations. Women feared for their lives and submit to men in fear. They became marionettes of a system which imprisoned young girls. It was established that light skin was good and black skin bad and the black community foolishly owned up to this believe and advertise it through their culture and entertainment. Making fun of their blackish challenges, embracing the disguise evil deeds of the world as their own personal trademarks. They create music that disrespect women and motherhood. And sold them as sex slaves on entertainment platforms. The poor disorientated mind of the young female accepted the abuse and bought into the lie. No longer did they cover their sacred bodies. No longer was there a need to follow custom and tradition. They played right in the hands of the one deceiving the world. While all along he was raising his daughters as the perfect opposite from the black girl. Yes, the great plan of deception had all its tracks covered. If the boy child would not train for army, he would be disrupted by the brutal black streets or conditioned by male clergy to embrace femininity. If he outsmart those three they would train him up and with their set of education he would become the puppet who invents scientific wonders under the names of the great masters, he would become the politician sodomizing his people to enrich himself and the grand master, or he would become the clergyman or lawyer enforcing the very laws that suppressed human sanity. The educated were scattered all over the place. Equip with knowledge and power, conditioned by the world on conscious levels. Entirely caught up by the deceit, cloth in greed that resembles gold yet highly disillusioned. By now Ishtar's head was spinning, every time she was trying to see beauty her eyes looked into a scene that challenged her sanity. Her eye looked again deep into the heart of another community. She was greeted with brutal evidence of how women were treated by the men who claimed to love them.

It was Friday afternoon, the 31 of August 2019, music roared from every street corner. Month-end symbolized happiness in the township. Merriments were at the order of the day, by 10 am, people would flood the supermarkets to compete in the rush of sales. It was a norm that all prices dropped on the known payday circles in the country; the 15th, 20th, 25th and 30th was known as the "combo specials" in grocery stores. But, everything wasn't about food because grocery stores obtained licenses to sell alcohol to the public. All of a sudden, everyone had access to alcohol at discounted prices. Access was given to everyone and no identity number checks were done to determine if the client was of age to purchase alcohol and cigarettes. The energy of celebration freely flowed all over the country. In this particular little town, it was no different. Boys as young as 14 years dodged school to smoke herb and drink alcohol in the riverbeds. Girls wore tight-fitting jeans, tiny shorts, and revealing clothes to entertain older men at the car wash. Car wash, oh, what a laugh it was at the thought of dancing, drinking and smooching next to a wet car and streaming soapy water. The idea of a car wash first started out as a small business initiative where unemployed young men opted to make money at an affordable price at locations closer to home rather than the big industrious labor market. To attract clients, loud music was played and this didn't only attract clients with cars but all the young and energetic beings to "socialize" at those spots. Very soon it operated as entertainment joints and cars were, in fact, randomly selected for a wash. Major entertainment clubs and disco joints closed down as the car wash phenomena reach it's peeked both in sales and entertainment. Local businesses were booming and soon, those with money and power opened their own replicas. The township life changed. In the past for a man to woe a lady, it was a norm to take her out to a decent restaurant in the city center, feed her some unknown delicacies, and watch tear-jerking movies at the cinema. In the township, on money challenged days he would call her out for a chat at the street corner, hustle for a kiss and hug under a hidden tree, out of sight of the elders but safe enough for her to run home. The girl would be at home at decent hours. With the introduction of the notorious car wash, which was located close to the houses, schools, and churches there was no need to go into the city. For a reasonably price, vetkoek, meaty soup and a couple of shared beers, the dating scene changed. Everything happened at close range. Parents tried to discipline the children because in Alkebulan, the understanding was that you were each other's keepers but with modern believes and laws, Ubuntu was no more. The Arab merchants entered the market and introduced the hubbly bubbly. Roaming the streets, hissing and puffing smoke all day in daylight. A substance that was known by the Middle Eastern men and used during respected hours became the new abused toy in the little town of Tsuams. The roads became unsafe and the girl was no longer safe. Her eye saw money and entertainment close to her home. The quiet nights of storytelling, family time and prayer was soon disturbed by loud music and peace never knew its place again in the township. Every second house was turned into a shebeen or a restaurant selling something. There was a constant movement in the streets day and night. Township locations that were demarcated and easily monitored by elders were infiltrated by strangers of other areas. Soon, people didn't know who was coming or going. Kids became clever, instead of being close to home, they would wander off to neighboring areas where they could freely indulge in substances that were prohibited at home. Far away from the all-seeing eyes of the elders. Soon, the parent gave up to war with the child in the street. It was no longer safe to tell a child his wrong and even give him/her a nice old fashion beating to instill discipline. Parents were outraged by the new governing laws implemented; such as children's rights which were never heard of on Alkebulan soil and each parent chose to educate and raise his own differently. Lifestyle, in general, became worse and the dark evil of disobedience towards the universal principles flew out the door. Crime increased and soon everyone was terrorized and robbed from decent peace and human co-existence. Men lost respect for women and soon atrocities worse than the animal kingdom were reported.

It was during such celebratory day that Silva took his girlfriend Mandy to the entertainment house. They had no car to wash but Silva was paid and in high spirits; the perfect surrounding of friends and cheap food for his lady of the night to be convinced that she is in the care of a moneymaker. She would not lack and he would be able to pay. The atmosphere was merry and the drinks flow in abundance because it was not only Silva's money but, a contribution of his friends too. There was an unofficial rule that those seated on the same table would contribute towards the night's supply of drinks. Very soon, the merriment escalated into a jealous rage as the men started competing for the attention of Mandy. Drunkenness had no understanding of chivalry and Mandy was caught up in the middle. She learned at Silva's hand the confusion of jealousy, rage and a different form of love. At one point, she would be scolded of being unfriendly and another, he would demand that she be considerate to his friend's needs. She kept on with his abuse and seasonal goodness because the greater hand of poverty was lingering above her sanity. She had three children with Silva and was unemployed. He was a good man and cared for his children. They didn't lack anything or so it seemed to the public eye. However in the silence of their bedroom chambers, which was an extension of the main house and far from the ears of the children, he would beat her in anger her. He was strategic and never left marks on visible places. Always hitting her where the clothes would hide the marks. She kept it hidden from family and friends and never complained.

That night, they enjoyed like any normal couple but Mandy could see the change in Silva's eyes. He kept watching her and soon started dropping hints of his dissatisfaction. Out of fear, she asked that they go home earlier than planned. The next morning, Mandy was no were to be found. The kids searched with their father everywhere. Soon, family and friends came to assist in the search but to no avail. Mandy was gone. The police set out search parties and the entire neighborhood was under heavy surveillance. For two full months, the search went on and the police gave up later. Just as everyone was settling in with acceptance that Mandy's funeral procession takes place without a body, shattering news reached the family. A haggard body was found in a river 25km from the location where they were living. An autopsy showed that Mandy was raped and cut up in pieces. The first suspect was Silva and, after months in jail without bail, he was found guilty and sentenced to life imprisonment. The society was perplexed. Never in the history of Namibia were such atrocities reported. People did not know what to make of it all and new speculations started as trust was broken and in-laws fought endlessly. The kids were torn between loyalty towards a loving father and the monstrous killing of their mother. Civil society and various governing bodies started raising awareness for domestic violence, substance abuse and various ills within the communities. However, it seemed as if an unknown door of hatred and evil was opened and everything moral fell apart. Years later, Mandy's children, two girls and three boys, were labeled as the "kids of the woman that was killed by their father". With mounting pressure of survival and searching for answers which no one could provide, the children later dropped out of school. The girls became pregnant at teen ages just like their mother and the boys went off to the street to fight for survival.

Would we say that it was the beginning of acts beyond reason or just an episode that lifted a ban from the silent instances in the lives of people? Whichever way, the following years proofed that more and more rape cases were reported. Women were raped and mutilated, children were abducted and murdered. Mutilation took the front lead and the illicit trade of alcohol and drugs enjoyed privileges men did not have. Governments bought into all sorts of corruption selling their countries and natural resources to the highest bidder in a quest to become rich. They were not concerned about the people. They ruled with the sole purpose of wealth creation. It was never about the people, never about the land, never about the future but all about their immediate need for luxurious lifestyles before dying. To this world, there was no afterlife. The leaders believed in nothing, even the atheist scorned them, because they at least believed that God did not exist; something that the current leaders did not have as they lived for the moment. Anarchy took over the country which was once known as the peaceful hub of Alkebulan and the few inhabitants remained silent. A few demonstrations here and there, a social media outcry and the wearing of black clothes to show solidarity became a norm but never a solution. The great action to curb the malice remained dormant and more and more female bodies hit the ground. Every social ill was given a name. The people learned about corruption, child pornography, human rights, and the latest; passion killings. It was better to give a name to the source and simply toss it aside until the next election time to brainwash people that their concerns were heard. In other parts of the piece of dirt called the world, it was no different. Each and every day a soul was departing from its host because of one or the other misfortune tossed upon people. The war was against each other, destroying the borrowed bodies and their habitat. They killed each other in the name of power; power which they did not understand, as that worth was not in their hands.

The rape and mutilation of the women was just the beginning of many. Some said the men were crazy, others called it a sad case of passion love and subsequent killing but a few referred to it as part of an emerging culture of human trafficking, Increasingly, body parts were sold on the black market for ridiculous prices and the greedy, smell the rot. All these happened in a country which was gripped under a pandemic which was linked to sex. A new virus (HIV) was discovered which was either transmitted through blood or sexual contact. The bacterium HIV could lead to full blown AIDS if not treated. It spread like wildfire through the world with most deaths reported from the motherland. Theories were propagated that the virus originated from the Alkebulanian ape and later transferred to its people. Other theories blamed it on the Western powers but all in all, the virus was there, stayed with the people for the last two decades and with retroviral drugs and lifestyle changes became manageable. When the virus broke out many people succumbed due to lack of treatment and knowledge of the disease but as with every challenge which came their way, the people of Alkebulan also found a remedy for the virus. Notwithstanding to mentioned that though some remedies were from natural herbs and thus effective, there were also those that came up with hazardous ideas to destroy others, amongst them were the people that believed that the virus could be healed through having sex with virgins. This sole belief let to countless rape cases on the continent. Research upon research was carried out to find a cure for the disease as the pandemic span out of control and this led to a new discovery in Alkebulan. Scientist found evidence that a certain group of women in Kenya were immune to the virus. Though the survey was conducted amongst women in the profession of sex, some wiser minds explored the possibility that the immunity may be found in other women with the same genetic features which would therefore include all Alkebulan nations. By studying the Alkebulanian female anatomy and comparing certain specimens they hoped to create antidotes for those carrying the virus. Or that was the type of propaganda release for Alkebulan and other parts of the world to believe. During the early explorations of continent, men from the west and east both discovered the special capabilities of the Alkebulan people. They knew what their skin and body were capable off. They also found their weaknesses of trust and gullibility and bank on it. This opened an avenue for scientific discoveries, one after the other were made on Alkebulan soil without the notice of its inhabitants. The explorers were disguised as missionaries, as blue bloods who escape their own revolutionary slaughter houses, as commoners trying to set up home elsewhere, as life would direct. None of them coming with the obvious agenda of owning the land and its people.

Ishtar looked at the world and sighed. Many a times, looking at the mess created, thoughts came to mind to simply wipe the entire species of the face of the earth. It was going to be much simpler. Amma could off course re-create another species if he needed. But during such a time, she would be reminded of the covenant which bounds Amma to these species. She would be reminded of the special bond between them and the promise which hold them accountable. At that moment of weakness, Ishtar's eye saw into the near future. A future were women where rising to take back control. Yes, they were getting into politics and mastering skills to outweigh men in power but, these were not the women she saw. Ishtar looked into the first house of an abusive husband, where there was a woman, scared and damaged by the man she once loved and adored. She knew him since her secondary school days. He treated her like a queen. "You are my queen", he would say to her on many occasions. "To your parents you are a princess but I see qualities of a queen in you. The woman who will make my house an enchanted space of love and joy. A mother to my children and keeper of peace. I will love and protect you." She believed him and married him. Her parents received a dowry that made their neighbours' envy rise. Her friends jealously unfriend her. But as soon as the bliss started with the birth of their first daughter, the evil eye introduced her husband to a new world of misplaced manly ego, teaching him that being a devoted husband was a disgrace to manhood. Soon, alcohol and abuse entered their house. The wife, taught by her parents to be submissive, remained silent. The elders' council couldn't help her, for they believed he was being manly. Her friends laughed behind her back. The society fearfully praised and included him amongst the circle of "good, powerful men". He rose in power and his businesses thrived. The daughters of the house increased to three. The beatings on the beautiful body temple of the wife never ceased until she could feel no more pain. Her daughters' would always flee to the elderly woman next door for safety. The husband kept abusing her and made her out as nothing. In his eye and that of his friends she became worthless thought she reasoned with esteemed intelligence. Although her parents were poor, she obtained bursaries and complete her first degree with a first class pass while her husband came through with an ordinary economics degree. She was ready for the engineering field, but her love for the only man she knew all her life stopped her in her tracks. She became a shadow of her old self. Even when she presented him with a male child, it was far gone. Outside the walls of their house, he was feeding sons born out of lust who were never his own. All fathered by his friend through the multiple women they shared each night at wild parties. The friend presenting him to the world as the master polygamist. The friend was deceiving him such that he was to end destroy his home, marriage and business, yet the husband didn't notice. Unfortunately friends like that were just many on the continent harming society and destroying happy homes and the system never caught up with them because such acts were in favour of the master manipulator's plan.

It was all planned out, when husbands died before their wives, they would be blamed. That was the new acceptable norm in Alkebulan. If his family were to be erased they would blame it on witchcraft and husband would commit suicide out of shame, disgrace or guilt. But the wife rose before all that could happen. One day when the friend brought home her husband completely drunk and carrying food in a parcel and a crate of beers in the other hand she knew that she had to turn things around. She watched the two arranging chairs outside and went out to help. She took the food from them, went inside the house and served it in decent plates. She brought it to them, presented them with a bucket to wash their hands and went inside. Both men were caught by surprise. The woman, begging her husband to stop drinking or the one which would grab her children and run next door was no more. The friend recovered first and laughed at her actions, but that single act brought back a glimpse of memory to her husband. She watched him from the window as he sat with a bowed head. Then later she returned with her best glasses, knelt next to her husband and poured him a drink. Then she presented another to his friend. Surprised and amused the friend took his drink while asking her. "What are you trying to achieve through all this?" Looking up to him, she answered boldly. "Nothing, I was taught to respect my husband, to serve him and be his companion. To be submissive to his vision for the family. I married a good man in the eyes of the community and instead of doing what I was supposed to do, I allowed the society to rob him from us and himself. I am a protector, a wife and mother. In the understanding of misplaced love, I forgot to show him the true essence of marriage, respect and love. I nearly succumbed to the fits of betrayal of that which is supposed to be gentle. Today, I simply surrender to the open understanding of defeat so that those in the world would see my husband rise to the true calling of his soul. I thus serve you friendship as only my husband can give. I serve you today an open welcoming to our house only as my husband can give. I serve you our well of care and understanding as only my husband can give. To him I serve loyalty, respect and love that surpasses all understanding only as a wife can give. So, welcome to our house until such time that my husband the man I married because of the wisdom he carried in his soul returns". Then she withdrew to the house. The friend still amused and laughing, the husband silent. She went into the living room and silently signaled her daughters to her side. Took the baby out of his cot and placed him in the arms of the eldest daughter. She then showed them towards the back door. A gesture understood by her daughters that it was time to flee. While watching her children rush over to the neighbour's house, a thought came to her mind that it may possibly be the last time. Then she turned around, knowing full well that this time she has overstepped her boundaries and went to the bathroom. If he had to beat her today, she thought, it would be without traces of blood. She was to stand up for her daughters even if it was by way of hiding her blood and face. She stripped off her clothes and went into the shower and fell on her knees as tears streamed down her face. After what felt like eternity she heard the first loud bang of a door. Shivers ran down her body. Her daughters also heard the sound as it vibrated all the way. They all listened and waited, but there was silence. The wife opened the tap so that water flowed on her body. She waited and heard him approaching. She didn't look up and just waited, her body tense and in fear. He came up close and touched her. He could feel how tense she was under his fingers and started to caress her body. First starting with her neck and shoulders, he kept on easing her body with his hands to relax, releasing the tensions slowly. She remained uncomfortable until she realized that no beating was coming forth. As she started relaxing under his hands, the husband turned her around to face him. Raised her head and looked into her eyes. She saw a transformed man and recognized him, the one with few words and kindness in his eyes. She saw the tears on his face. With her eyes, she embraced him back into her heart. Without words, he saw forgiveness and love and he took her to know her better than before. An hour passed yet they kept on and on. He needed to delve into the depth of her being. Not just to reclaim her body but to connect with her and join in spirit. She let him be and they fulfilled the promise of love that night. Much later he lifted his wife's exhausted body out of the shower and took her to the bedroom. There he put her gently on the bed, covered the fragile beautiful body for the first time in years with a bedsheet and sat by her until she dozed off. Then he dressed himself and went out in search of his children. The old lady next door looked at him and also saw the new birth. She smiled reassuring to the kids and sent them home with him. At home he held hugged them all with tears flowing down his cheeks and pleaded for forgiveness. That night he made a clumsy dinner and fed his children before retiring to bed. The girls were not convinced. Since they returned, they didn't hear a sound from their parents' room. Let alone saw their mother. The girls looked around suspiciously and went along with their father's new behaviour cautiously. They even suspected him of possible homicide as they couldn't justify his reformation. The girls stayed awake until late that night because they wanted to investigate the matter. When they thought it was safe enough, they snuck down the corridor to their parents' room. Their dad left the door deliberately opened as he could see how cautious his daughters' were around him that night. A simple way of reinforcing trust. The girls peeped through the open door just to find their mother sleeping peacefully where she belonged on their father's chest. The girls watched in total shock and as they stood there, understood for the first time what the old woman next door told them. "There would come a day that your mother will wake up to the wisdom greater than herself". They looked and understanding dawn on them. As the girls were returning with happy smiles and a bright expectation for tomorrow on their faces, the first light worker closed her door next door. She moved swiftly and switched off all the lights and came to a standstill in the middle of the living room. With her head raised to the ceiling, she banged her feet on the floor. The floor opened immediately beneath her feet and the old lady alight the stairs made visible by an unseen light.

Work was beginning and Ishtar was happy. Her eye moved to a second location where a small girl was playing in the street with her friends, not far from the house of her aunt. The little girl was lured away by her uncle's friend with a promise that he was going to buy her sweets and many gifts at a shop at the mall not far from the house. He would always bring presents and sweets for her thus she trusted him. When she heard that they were going to the mall she was excited and called her friends to follow them. Usually, the uncle wouldn't mind but on this particular day he refused that the others accompany them. Explaining to the little girl that it was a special day, he said he wanted to spoil her alone as her birthday was approaching and he may not be able to celebrate with them. Hence buying her gifts in advance, and she had the privilege of going with him to pick any gift of her choice. "We should go alone but you can tell everyone and show them the gifts only once we return. The little girl followed him reluctantly. Well, it was customary. In Alkebulan, children were raised in an open community. They played everywhere as it was safe to roam around the entire suburbs. All elders both male and female where their parents. They trusted each elder with the same regard they had for their biological parents that's why it didn't matter if they spend days at a relative's house instead of their parents own. On top of it all, she knew the uncle very well. He was a friend to his uncle and frequently visited her aunt's house. Sometimes her uncle would joke that he spends more time at their house instead of his own. She also knew how to behave towards strangers. Her mother taught her very well, thus at the age of 9, she was able to identify strangers from friends and family. Her parents were at peace and the neighbours too. They all trusted her intelligence at such a young age. It wouldn't be the first time either for her to go to the mall with a grown up other than her uncle or aunt, they had many friends and extended family and they all treated as their own. As they were walking down the street, neighbours and friends recognized and greeted them both. At intervals, the uncle's friend would stop and have a brief talk with one or two people before proceeding. Later, they got to the taxi rank and took a cab to the mall situated at the other side of the location. The man chose the mall located close to a river bed and instead of being dropped off at the mall entrance, he asked the driver of the cab to live them at the bridge leading to the mall across a river bed. From there the little girl could see the mall and was very excited. Upon her inquiry as to why they had to get off the cab so far, he simply said that he liked to walk over the bridge while observing the beautiful sight of the river. He also knew that the girl loved birds and said to her that they could first watch some of the birds nesting in the riverbed before crossing over to the mall. She agreed and they walked down with the footpath and when they approached the middle he stopped abruptly. "Can you hear that strange sound?" he asked the girl. "Yes, it's a sound of a bird" she exclaimed. "Uncle, can we please search for it, please can we?" she begged him. As that was the expected reaction he agreed and led the little girl deeper into the river which was covered by tall grass and huge trees. The town received good rains over the past couple of weeks thus the trees and grass around the river bed were flowing lovely and it was indeed filled with birds with different colours. As the girl jumped and played around with excitement, the man started to prepare himself. While talking to her, he removed gloves from his pockets and put them on. Patiently he allowed the girl to play and exhaust herself while he was seating and waiting on large stone nearby. Just as children have it, she was soon bored and remembered the reason why they left the house; her gift. She rushed over to the man and sat down next to him. As she turned around to tell him that it was time for them to go to the shop, he covered her mouth and nose with a handkerchief dipped in an anesthetic substance. The girl collapsed into his arms immediately. With a grin, he picked up the small body and moved into the part where the trees were densely populated and out of sight and laid her down. Then he ran towards another bush and brought out a bag which he had hidden there. From the bag he removed sanitizers and a set of knives and placed them nearby the girl. Everything was done with precision as if performing a ritual. Slowly, he cleaned the knives and laid them bear for use. Then he undressed the little girl and picked up one of the knives. He shifted himself on one knee and was about to cut her throat when a warm feeling moved down his spine. He swung around in surprise because there no one was supposed to be in that part of the bushes. He took days to observe the movement of people around the bridge and concluded that only few men made use of the bridge. With the increase in crime rates, people, mostly women, avoided such places. Thus, he was surprised to see the person standing behind him. However, there was no time, whatever she hit him with cut deep into his back and was straining his body. He dropped slowly on top of the girl as blood started streaming down his back. The person behind tossed him off the little girl and knelt next to her. She then removed a herbal mix from her pockets and blew some into the air in close proximity with the girls face. This ignited the girl's senses and she started drifting back to consciousness. The little girl opened her eyes and saw what laid before her. When she looked up, they locked eyes and the woman put a finger on her lips to indicate to the child to remain silent. She dressed her quickly and picked her up. As she walked with the girl back to the roadside. By the time they got back with a taxi, people and police were running all around the street in search. It was getting dark by then and when the aunt realised that the girl was nowhere to be found, they called the police to assist in a search. The woman got off the car at the corner of the street. She paid her dues and walked with the girl still in her arms up the road towards the girls' family home. People stood by stunned by the scene unfolding before their eyes. This was the lady everyone called a witch. She was ridiculed because of her disabled state and never left her home or interacted with the community members. Children were afraid of her and no one except the little girl she was holding in her arms would visit her. The girl would always share her sweets with the lady and play with her birds. Asking why she kept them in a cage. She walked with the girl slowly to their home without being intimidated by the people closing in around them. She was beyond their insults, off course some still hurled insults while others were just curious were she was coming from holding the child so dear in her arms. When they reached the house she walked straight to the mother and placed the child in the weeping mother's arms and left without a word. That night as the little girl woke up from her induced sleep she, recounted the day's story to the parents and family. Her uncle informed the police and a search party was sent to the river. There they found the bracelet of the little girl, the footprints of three people confirming the girl's story. Uncles' friend was unconscious at the time a witness found and took him to the hospital. Doctors pronounced him paralyzed and wheelchair bound for the rest of his life due to the severity of the injury. The witness vanished, the attacker of the man vanished, only the little girl knew who saved her life. That night the lady opened the bird cage, released her three birds and went inside her dark house. Another light worker exiting the space of humans.

Ishtar was encourage as the light workers were popping up everywhere to help. Her eye shifted to another house, where a mother sat in tears. She joined the church at the tender age of 18. Mesmerized by the words of salvation which were preached from the pulpit she eagerly fed at the feet of her spiritual fathers. Over the years, she worked for the church and learned to grow her faith. During her early adulthood as many an occurrence seen in the local establishment of her church, she was singled out by a few woman and placed on a journey of becoming a wife. Visions were received and many confirmed that she was to marry a well-known clergy and she followed suit. For her mother's in the church were wise prayer warriors and their word was respected. Two years of supposed marital bliss fell into an awakening of life. The supposed performance in the bedroom was challenged and the husband constantly searched for pleasures outside. Teachings from the elders in church and her traditional upbringing was of such that you don't speak outside the bedroom and involve people with your worries. She was advised to seek guidance from God and remain prayerful. Her lifestyle was soon consumed of daily prayer and meditation, though at times her thoughts would hinder her to go out and investigate what her husband was doing. She followed him one night and had a devastating revelation. The clergy man was visiting gay night clubs and engaging with men. Upon questioning, he denied and her prayer partners laughed and gossiped about her affairs at home. Hurt by the church people she trusted she turned away from it all and concentrated on solving her household issues alone. Through mutual connections and exposure back into the 'non-religious' world, she found answers of how to fight for her husband. Following paths from witchdoctors back to brothels, she tried everything in an effort to keep her husband. Because in the eyes of the world surrounding her. If a man seeks attention outside the house, it was not regarded his fault but rather because the women was not able to satisfy his needs. Again, the African culture alluded that he was entitled to many woman. In her case the husband went to other men instead of women. This was a societal taboo. Customs were very strict in their ways of raising sons and daughters such that those that felt different would either hide or not disclose their sexual preferences. The information about male sexual orientation was also ridiculed and misinformed. In loose terms they were called degrading names and made out as the worst sinners by the church. With all that going, she didn't feel encouraged to approach anyone for help. She gave birth to two children yet that didn't keep her husband at her side. He left home and she carried on with her children. Though he left, he remained a supportive father and the kids grew up in both houses of their parents. Years later, a second tragedy reached her doorsteps; both her children informed her that they were gay. The news nearly destroyed her as she couldn't feel encouraged to face another trial against the world to defend her children. She loved them dearly and raised them in a befitting manner. They lead ordinary lives and she wasn't sure where she went wrong. At times she wondered if the exposure to their dad's lifestyle was to be blamed. On other occasions science assured her that it was a biological occurrence. Her sad question remained why her house was targeted. Her children were mocked and ridiculed and the church finally scrapped her from all titles she held dearly. Her ministry and gift of healing was frown upon and she couldn't engage with anyone in the community with ease. Her children saw all this and the guilt build up in their spirits. One night her son returned from a night out with bruises; evidence of the negative perception of the society they lived in. As he narrated, some of his friends took him out to a party and introduced him to some men. One of the man showed interest in him and led him on. He followed the man outside the party house, just to find that it was a trap. The others were waiting outside and they all beat him that night. If not for the assistance of a strange woman, he would've bled to death. That night upon hearing what happened to her brother, the girl committed suicide. The strange woman came to their house during the memorial service. There were only ten close friends all throughout the memorial service, everyone else was afraid to be associated with the family. For there was a time in the past that LGBTQ+ people were accepted. However, as the tide was turning and everyone searching for a reason why the continent was in disarray, they were blamed. Alkebulanians were proud people with strong religious practices as inherited from the slave masters. They believed that only one sexual orientation was godly and all else was sin. Thus, the first target after fighting their liberation wars was against all things foreign. Hence, including LGBTQ+ people. The stranger looked deeply in the eyes of the defeated mother and asked if she wishes to live in a country far removed from negativity such as the one she was experiencing. She answered affirmative and that night, holding her limping son, she followed the strange lady through a tunnel under her house which she wasn't even aware existed.

Although some things were indeed foreign to the Alkebulanian tradition and way of life. It was humbling to witness how they embraced change within the societies. They believed that anything which could be named in native languages was identifiable and had roots to justify its existence. Thus embracing the new forms of life. This made Ishtar happy and with resigned peace she looked into another house, when on a fine day the husband disappeared, leaving his wife and children to fend for themselves. The mother stepped up to the responsibility and took two jobs to support her family. They were leaving in a notorious location governed by gangs and drug lords. The entire atmosphere was not conducive as there was a huge lack of male role models. Boys were dropping out of school to join gangs and push drugs. Mothers were overworked, tired and constantly worried about the safety of their children. Girls were pressured into earlier sexual activities. Under such pressures the woman was left by her husband but she stepped up to protect and provide for her children. She managed her home and disciplined her children such that there was order and decency. Instead of being encouraged they were ridiculed on the streets. Called names that they were trying to copy white lifestyles and all. However, she kept her ground, praying every day that the life on the street didn't crept into her home. Those were challenging days because the absence of a father meant she had to play both roles for her children and groom her sons on her own to become better men in the future. As the boys were growing, she could see their frustrations for the conditions under which they lived. They didn't approve how hard their mother was working to provide for their needs. Each night assuring her that they would work hard and complete their schools to be able to take care of her. The mother strained by the responsibility to care for her two sons while trying to hold two jobs down to pay for their living expenses. Unfortunately before that day could come, her last born was gunned down at the street corner while walking back from the shops. The family was devastated and filled with rage and the eldest son vow to avenge his death. The woman pleaded each day, trying to make her son see reason. However he slipped out of range and eventually joined the street gangs. Each night standing by the window, she would panic at every sound gunshots and feet running. She would pray with open eyes while watching through the window for each and every boy out in the streets until one night, she decided to take the battle by the horns and venture out into the dark streets looking for her son. As she walked along the pavement not knowing where to start her actual search, the boys would recognize her and greet her with humble submission. She asked after her son and soon got directions to a rundown place which was apparently his castle. She learned on the way that he little boy turned into one of the mightiest man on the street and this puzzled her because he was the gentle one between her two sons. Though they didn't get an entire clear report, she could vow that the late brother might have stubbornly offended someone, but in their type of society, there were codes of silence and no one could tell her what truly transpired on that day. But to learn on the streets that her gentle son turned into a feared thug was beyond her senses. She eventually found him in a dark ally of the castle. Drugged and sleeping in a corner. With the helped of two other boys she carried her son home that night. For three days in a row he slept and when he finally woke up her saw insanity in his eyes. Growing up in the hood she walked with her ears on the ground and could tell immediately that her son either took a substance he never used or that someone else drugged him with something that didn't agree with his system. Otherwise the excessive use of drugs over the past two years may have let him to insanity. She didn't know anything about mental health or about what was prescribed in the world to treat it and also get the person off drugs. At the same time she was deeply shamed by everything she learned that night. With stubborn motherly instincts she decided to make a plan. With the assistance of a carpenter, she cut out a wooden piece from his door, erected burglar bars and locked her son inside. Swearing that day to the heavens that she was going too fast and pray until she gets healing for her son. For days they stayed under lock and key. The boy screaming from the withdrawal symptoms he was having from the drug abuse and losing his mind due to pains. She fed him water and food through the opening in the door. His room started stinging from urine, vomit and fesses but she kept him under lock and key. Sitting at night next to his door and crying with him, calling out to the Lord to save her son while fearing at times that he would succumb to death because of the pains he was going through but stubbornly keeping to the promise that she was not going to lose another son. The neighbours would knock on her door out of concern but she never answered. They would call police but she would refuse to open her door. Church groups would come by and her workplaces would call. To this mother nothing else mattered other than to safe her son from the streets. After the first huddle was over she started talking to her son. Telling him that she didn't know what he would get up to in the streets but by her recollection of street life and the information about his status she paint a picture so horrible for him to listen too. Telling him that, that person people descripted was not her son, as she has raised a gentle soul. One that cared about people and couldn't hurt a soul. A boy who would speak to the elderly with respect and carry their groceries for them from the shops. A boy who believed in his mom's prayers. Thus explaining to him that all the other mother's whose children were on the streets were equally praying the same prayers she would for their children. Painting a vigil picture of how he was destroying lives of others and murdering people as if he was going to bring back his brother to life. Together while keeping him under lockdown and herself sitting by his door, they prayed together and shared memories of bygone days. By then use to the disgusting smell in the house coming from his room. Precisely two months later she emerged with her son from the house. Load their car with all their belongings and drove out of the town, ready to start a new live elsewhere. Six months later they were hosted by a family that owned a rehabilitation center where both of them served to try and save lives. Thus two light workers walking out of the experiences to serve lives.

It was not only the unfortunate which were lead out of different cities. Ishtar's eye wondered to another scene where those standing in good services for the world yet getting frail as age overtook them, were equally led out of the space by the light workers. All across the continent the work she was send for to complete has started. Obviously it was not in huge numbers that light workers operated an exodus but the gentle work they carried out was noticed. There however was a need to increase the numbers before people succumbed to the wars and strange diseases which were released by Memnon and his followers. She looked within and asked if she was truly ready to destroy all that. Ishtar sighed and smile. No, she can't destroy the world, nor can Amma. He loved it too much, nor can

Memnon, he didn't really understand it all. Her eye then moved to another set in a school class. Where a certain girl was busy writing examinations. Copying answers from her phone whenever the invigilator turned his head. She was one of the newly breed sly queens of the town. They were a new breed of young women using men to advance their livelihood and career aspirations. While her friends were out there engaging in the old form of the hailed profession. She decided to go back to school to advance her education. Education which was financed by the many suitors she had. There were those responsible for her school fees, others for accommodation in the city center and another for food and clothing, even some for entertainment and classy traveling. She played the game expertly. But she hungered for more as competition was fierce. While she was in school missing time out, some of her colleagues were flourishing financially buying cars, apartments and opening business which were all funded by influential men. She wanted that but knew that she had to complete her studies even if it was by cheating, buying and copying assignments and all. She was writing her final test and knew that she would graduate with flying colours. It was for this purpose that the faculty dean was her treasured client for the last six months prior to final exams. Well, the society may scorn and ridiculed her. Her mother also put her out of the house when she refused to mend her ways. So she was all alone, hustling in her own way. Reasoning that she wasn't killing anyone or selling drugs. She wasn't consuming any illegal substances either. A pure breed with a sound mind and good health because she took good care of herself. The men that paid for her services knew what they were buying. There were no expectations beyond it from both sides. They came out at free will, paid for what they received and moved on with life. None interfering in the other's personal lives. Just as she was finishing off a text message came in. She quickly read it, hide her phone in her bra and called the invigilator to collect the answer script. The urged her to meet her best friend outside the school gate. Today, she was to be introduced to one of the top businessmen of the country. The man was looking for an escort to accompany him on his numerous business trips. His wife was an ambitious woman building her own business brand and didn't have time to follow him only to sit in hotels and look beautiful for his pleasure and entertainment. The type of business he was involved in also required that he present himself as a trustworthy citizen thus an escort from his country would pass as the second wife. Alkebulanians were known to be polygamist thus no one would rise an eye brow if they saw a different woman by his side. Furthermore he believed that his illegal dealings won't be detected if he could cover them through a protected shield. The girl agreed. She had nothing to lose, in fact she won much more. Traveling overseas, staying in exotic hotels, wine and dinning with high flyers of the world. They travelled all over the world. Soon she discovered the type of businesses he was dealing in. Deals that involved many of Alkebulans high ranking government officials. The girl increased her rates but the man refused to pay. Thus she decided to increase her finances through other means. The constant traveling expose her to business opportunities and also exposed her to more potential clients both local and international. By engaging with them she also picked up on explosive evidence against the Alkebulanian officials of the entire continent which she didn't know how to handle. On a fateful day she discovered shuttering personal news. The news at the doctors was twofold. Being three months gone with a pregnancy and HIV diagnosed. She played and partied so hard that she didn't guard her period cycles and messed up her contraceptives. When she eventually realized that she was pregnant it was already too late to do something about it. Broken, she returned home. For the first time looking around her environment. Living in a rundown location, having smart furniture, phones and clothes. She had nothing tangible to fall back on. No savings, no privately owned apartments. At least she managed to buy over the period of two years but there was no time to invest into the actual business opportunities she was offered or save her money for rainy days. She was having too much fun running all around the world and living a glamorous lifestyle outside. Her official client promised to set her up with a business and a lump sum of money after two years thus she was not worried. But in between he learned of her exchanges with other men and distanced himself. She couldn't thus make him or any other men responsible for her pregnancy, let alone try and extort some money from any in her condition. They simply pushed her aside and found new girls to play with. Heartbroken and disillusioned she wondered around the streets begging from one friend to the other. She also tried looking for a job but though holding a two year old degree without experience and equally competitive labour market it was difficult. She sold her car to life on for a few months but things were expensive in the changing world and she couldn't manage. When her rent was due the landlord simply evict her. That fateful day, siting by a corner wondering where to go, she met a lady who was looking for a domestic worker. She followed her home and was offered the servants' quarters to live in. Her pregnancy couldn't allow her to do much but her new employer didn't mind. The lady informed her that she was an orphan and promised to help her and the unborn child. She further promised to help her find a suitable job once she was put to bed. Unfortunately in the seventh month of the pregnancy she developed complications and died during an emergency child birth. Prior to her demise she shared all the things she observed during her travels with the lady. Not only did she relate information but also told her were to find the damning evidence she hid for the past two years. The lady went to the girls' old house and retrieve everything. There were copies of sales agreements, copies of money transfers, and pictures of those involved. For solid two months the lady spent investigating and writing articles and sending it to different news channels all around the world. Each week there was breaking news from one channel after the other. Unveiling the biggest crime syndicates master minded by the high ranking government officials. There were undocumented sales of natural resources, money laundering, drug trafficking, prostitution and human trafficking. High ranking officials from many countries in Alkebulan were caught with their pants down. Presidents were firing ministers left right and center to cover their tracks when implicated. Chaos erupted all over in political circles. Foreign investors implicated were either forced to resign or committed suicide to avoid jail sentences. Some even closed doors against international trade with Alkebulan. The continent's leaders were left hanging. Some admitting guilt, some committing suicide but the majority covered by diplomatic immunity and simply moved on with life without any guilt. As old age had it they soon started getting sick and dying 'natural' deaths. Never once was it recorded that any high ranking official all over Alkebulan died of HIV related deaths. But yet again a light worker revealed the power of silent warfare as she held the child born out of greet and irresponsibility and lead him to a new world.

For the next couple of days Ishtar's eye wondered all around Alkebulan. From the impressive houses of the rich and mighty to the impoverished tents of the destitute. She saw corruption, deceit and malice at one side but it was all clouded by the pure hearts and hopefulness found in some of the people be they rich or poor through honest experiences in life. Though they have long cease from trusting their leaders. They continued to hustle to keep body and soul together as a nation. They prayed and the live with the hope that one day it would all change for the better. Oh yes, all citizens were not entirely honest either. Amongst them were also found those that carried sinister minds like their leaders. There were others that stole and kill in a quest to make themselves rich.

There were the jealous plotting night and day against the success of their neighbours. There were those breaking all cultural norms and spitting on tradition in their quest to embrace the foreign cultures. Admits all that there were also the gentle at heart, those that tried to build something out of the many nothings. Those that set up soup kitchens to feed children and the elderly. Those that volunteered to educate their people on social matters. There were equally many good projects working towards the reform of citizens of Alkebulan. And these were the people Ishtar needed to protect and guide on the sacred trail.

CHAPTER EIGHT

After observing all this scenes in the various communities through her third eye. It was time to unveil her powers. Ishtar was transported magically to another location in another town. The street was unusually quiet. There were no kids running around. No shouts of joy, laughter or even scolding mothers. It seemed like a scene from a thriller, from which a serial killer would suffice. She didn't know what to expect, let alone what to do, so she stood in that same place where she landed for a very long time. As the hours went on and the night creeped closer, she remained waiting and watching. The scene became more haunting but she kept waiting. A lone figure appeared by the far corner. She looked down the street and hesitantly step onto its threshold to walk further down. Slowly but surely she moved, one foot after the other. Instead of standing in the dark for protection she came to a standstill under a dim streetlight, while looking over her shoulder, then from house to house. The curtains were drawn close at each house. There was total silence. Not even one curious old lady peeping out to observe the stranger in the street. This was an unusual Saturday evening in the township and she was puzzled. Perhaps it was one of the new developments in town where the middle-class citizens were living because those ones were very quiet, unlike the notorious neighborhoods were noise was at the order of the day. She noted that developers were increasingly building housing estates for the affluent, which was far removed from hood. Houses with high wall fencing, electric gates, and governed by body corporates with rules that scared the ordinary person away. This may be a similar establishment Ishtar thought. The she started walking down the road with caution. Suddenly the lone figure she saw at the far end came running behind her. She froze in her tracks with a heart-pounding heavy.

"Run girl! Run!" he screamed

Without a second thought, Ishtar started running. The man overtook her at high speed and disappeared from sight. She didn't look left, right or even to the back where the man was coming from. After a few seconds, a bright light shone through the corner, followed by screeching sounds of wheels. She turned and saw a car approaching. Her instinct started taking over. She turned into another street and kept running. Without effort, her body picked up and increase her speed. The car was getting closer and closer. She kept running on high speed and turned into another street. Unfortunately just to find herself in a cul-de-sac. She stopped in her tracks contemplating how to turn back and run past the oncoming car. The houses surrounding her were all shut; brick walls, electric fences, and burglar wires were all staring back to her. Slowly Ishtar turned and look back in the direction of the approaching car. She knew without a doubt that her escape was through that same road. Her mind separated from her body. There was no more time for reasoning. She stopped thinking and acted according to the ideas forming in her mind, running back at full speed towards the car. The drivers in the car stepped on their breaks in shock. They didn't expect the girl to turn towards them and running back. They looked at each other to make a decision. But during that split second of doubt, they let their prey pass by them. The road was narrow and the car standing right in the middle of it. Ishtar's body simply carried her on top of the car and landed softly on the other side. Within a second, she accelerated and disappeared into another street. The two drivers in the car looked shocked at each other and quickly turn to pursue her but when they got to the turnoff, she was gone. This time Ishtar was not running in the streets. Her body was jumping fences and running on rooftops with ease. She was too confused to think or ask what was happening. So, she kept running until she got to a house slightly separated from the others. To her it seemed like the only house without a brick wall and she ran straight into the yard. As she was approaching someone opened the door and pulled her in. Breathless she landed inside on her knees. Looking around her.

"You will be safe here." Someone said to her and she relaxed. They brought water for her and watched her drink and rest. After some good minutes, she gathered her strength and rose from her knees. As she was regaining consciousness Ishtar looked around and saw that many people were cramped in the tiny room. The house where she was didn't resemble any of the beautiful mansions she was running past. This one seemed as if she was in the older part of town, where things were more run down and old. Yet the house was more secured with burglar bars and devices she could not identify than others.

"Where am I?" She asked the lady that opened the door for her.

"You are saved. We are all hiding here from the soldiers?"

"Yes, dear. The government took up arms against anyone that is not enlisted in the new movement. You know that don't you? She looked at Ishtar confused.

"No, no. I didn't know. In fact, I just got here today." She answered.

"From where?"

"Eh, eeeh. From ....eeeh." Ishtar looked at them equally confused. She didn't know and they could tell that much from her expression.

The lady looked stern at her and then turned to the others. She smiled and clapped her hands in amusement.

"Can't you see? She is from the other side. You all saw how she was jumping the fences effortlessly and running from one roof unto another as if she was flying. You all saw that right?"

The group of people started murmuring amongst each other with excitement. Ishtar couldn't make out what they were saying as they spoke in different languages. She turned back to the lady and asked where she was. Promising to explain everything the lady moved Ishtar out of the living room. She sat her down in another room and closed the door behind them. They sat for some time in silence, then the lady looked up and started talking. "We are caught up in a war many people don't understand. A few days ago, everything seemed fine and people were happy. Only the wise on eye could see the approaching danger while the foolish few refused to see. We therefore started to prepare." She narrated every evil Ishtar has been witnessing so far and explained that they discern the signs of war and change. She also explained that they were out to get people to safety all across Alkebulan. The corrupt leaders labelled them as rebels and pursued them but she explained to Ishtar that they were not out to rig elections or seek riches. They were only interested in saving the human race, to free the soul which was captured by the carnal body that lusted after the worldly things.

She sat silently for a while and Ishtar looked at her asking softly. "Am I from that world?" The lady jerked her head up and stared at Ishtar. She even rose from the chair and started pacing across the room. Why do you ask that question, I've seen you outside? No one in this world can do things you just did." She answered. "Does it mean that I'm part of your world?" Ishtar asked again. The lady stopped pacing and looked at Ishtar with concern.

You really don't know?

 No, I don't know but I found myself outside in the street. Someone ran passed me screaming that I too should run. Then a car chased after me as I was running. The next thing I knew, is that you opened your door for me. Slowly and smiling the woman started pacing the floor again. Wrapping her hands against each other and looking at the girl while thinking how it was possible that she didn't know anything. Oh my Lord, this is not possible, she really doesn't know! She jumped in excitement and quickly rushed out to inform the others.

"My people this is Ishtar. We were waiting for her. She is here now; our prayers have been answered by the gods." She said

Ishtar was surprised that the lady knew her name because she is sure that she didn't introduced herself but looking at the happy faces around her she decides to remain silent. A few minutes later, the older women shouted and for a moment they forgot about Ishtar.

"Close the curtains quickly. Someone get to the back door, close it quickly."

Heavy curtains were drawn to cover the windows and a door shut in the distance. Everyone sat quietly and not a sound was heard from inside. They sat for ten minutes then heard male voices outside.

"Her tracks ended at that house in front but we checked inside. There was no one there."

"Keep looking she can't be far. This is a dead-end, from here there is no other way out. Keep looking, remember the boss wants her alive."

"Why is this one special?"

"She was wearing a white dress you fool. When last have you seen someone in this city wearing white?"

"She could be new here."

"Exactly. That is why the boss asked that we bring her in for questioning. We need to know where she is coming from and why she's traveling alone."

People inside the house turned to look at Ishtar. Her dress was not white. She was wearing a golden dress but it was glowing. The men outside might have mistaken the glowing light for white. Quickly the old woman covered her with a blanket. Outside the men stopped in their tracks.

"I think I saw a light inside that house at the far end."

"Come let us get closer and investigate."

Inside the house, one of the men moved slowly towards a switch mounted on the wall and pressed on. To Ishtar's eye, nothing happened but the men outside felt the impact of whatever was switched on.

"It's too dark out here, are you sure you have seen a house?" Someone asked.

"Yes, there was a house right here. I'm sure."

"We know by now that there are a whole lot of unexplainable occurrences in this town nowadays. Pitch a sign here and we can check it out in the morning."

The people inside listened silently to all the movements and voices outside. Only when all sounds and talking faded away, they sighed with relief.

"Now we are trapped." Someone said.

"Yes indeed. They will see the house in the morning. We have no way of moving." The old woman said, but the one that opened the door to Ishtar was hopeful. She looked at Ishtar and said.

"No, we are not trapped. In fact, we have just been rescued. Let's all go to bed."

As it seemed, no one questioned her and simply obeyed her instructions. They all exchanged greetings and while others left to sleep elsewhere in the house, some just made themselves comfortable right on the floor where they were seated. The old woman had blankets packed next to her chair and walked around covering everyone. Then she settled into her own chair. Ishtar took her blanket, covered the old woman, and sat down next to her. The elder stretched out her hand and squeezed Ishtar fondly. That night, Ishtar drifted between sleep and dreams. Every other hour, she would wake with a shock, realize that she was dreaming and close her eyes again. The next morning, she woke up with familiar sounds around her. People were up and going around the day as usual. There were breakfast smells coming from the kitchen and children were playing outside. There was a merry air all around the house , so much so that even the curtains were drawn away from the windows. If not for the people around her Ishtar would have thought that she had a dream about the night before. However, everyone with her in the house proved enough that last night happened. She moved around the house, greeting and talking to everyone and later went outside and sat again next to the old woman at the front porch. The woman smiled but kept looking into the distance. After a while, she spoke.

"The men from last night are camping all around our house." She said. Ishtar looked around but could not see anyone. There were a few houses around theirs. The fancy houses were a few blocks away on the other side of the road. Where she was seated was definitely not affluence. The houses looked similar, there were no fancy fences and everyone had open access. On the left side, she saw a man and a younger boy cleaning their yard and another house looking all descent with a woman sweeping in front while her children were playing with a ball. The house on the far side had a man that was reading his morning paper on the porch. Nowhere could she see anyone suspicious, camping and watching the house.

"You are looking with the wrong eye." The old woman giggled and turned to Ishtar. That's when Ishtar realized with a shock that she was actually blind.

"You cannot see? Oh sorry, ma'am are you…"

"Yes child, I have been all my life."

"But, but last night? You were covering everyone with blankets. Even me."

"Yes, child. All of you look at the world with the wrong eye."

"What do you mean?"

"It's not for today. You will understand soon. Just keep listening to your inner being as you did last night, then, everything will be made clear. Now let's go inside the food has been served."

Ishtar just looked at the elder and smiled, indeed food has been served.

The day passed by fleetingly and soon the night drew near. It was with the approaching darkness that Ishtar saw the man in grey suits. It was the same men sitting at the porch, cleaning the yard and acting merry good family at their respective houses. Now as the wives closed the curtains and put kids to bed they emerged. They stood by their gates in grey suits, fully armed. Ishtar was now wondering if she was caught up in some kind of war zone. True to herself she didn't question but just moved inside the house with the others and immediately covered herself with a blanket. The three men walked over to their house by nightfall just as the first street lights were switched on. Everyone inside remained calm and collected. Only in the fidgeting hands of the younger ones, you could detect fear as the rest of the people remained calm. Some windows were still open to show the illusion of a peaceful house. The radio was switched on and the old lady was busy amending a cloth. Other than that, the entire house was silent. The men walked around doing what they did; investigating every little thing outside and then called to retreat. As they were walking away, one said.

"Everything seems alright. Apart from the new girl that joined them."

"Which girl, I didn't see any new faces during the day."

"There was one, she sat in a yellow dress all day long next to the blind old woman."

"Joshua! There was no one next to the old lady. I was sitting right in front of their house. I would have seen her and a yellow dress amongst all the black colors would have stood right out for me to notice."

"Nope, I know what I have seen. When the commander comes, I will ask for clearance to enter the house." With that said, they walked away.

"And they are all color blind too." The old lady said suddenly and everyone giggled. "Oh, they can't see your blue clothes and the little girl is wearing a golden dress." She chuckles softly. A man asks with concern in his voice. "Granny, what should we do? It's the first time that they decided to come to our house."

"Don't fear my son. You will all do what this little girl tells you to do."

Ishtar looked from the old lady to the others in complete shock. She did not know what to do either, let alone understand anything that was happening all around her. How could she, she didn't know why she was here and what powers were transferring her from one place to another.

The men came back that night and entered from the front gate. The old lady instructed everyone to close the curtains and cover Ishtar with a blanket. Her glow would have given them reason to enter the house. However, someone had forgotten to close the back door. They heard one of the soldiers screaming to the others to use that entrance. Footsteps rushed to enter through the back door. The old lady looked at Ishtar and said, "Now is the time for you to act. These people are here to be led by you." Hesitantly, Ishtar looked around. Then she screamed to everyone to enter the room close to the living room. Everyone scrambled into it and hurdled inside. She didn't know what to do. Someone in the crowd locked the room and soon they started moving furniture against the door. With the door secured and limited safety available, they all turned to her with expectation. The old lady came again towards Ishtar, placing her hands softly on her face. She started rubbing the sides of the face softly while talking. "Child, we all have gifts according to our purpose. Although my eyes can't see what the light emits, I can see what others cannot. The minute you stepped in, I knew that you were the one this group was waiting for. Now, start to believe in yourself." As she was talking, the soldiers were fast approaching. They were getting closer to the living room. "Find them quickly." Someone screamed. Next the electricity was cut and they were in darkness. They heard a voice at the door. "I heard footsteps shuffling in here." People were overcrowded inside and it was difficult for any to stand still. As the soldiers started to bang on the door, the old lady screamed to Ishtar. "Now!" Ishtar immediately removed the blanked and the room lit up. She went into a trance like state and started pacing the room quickly. Then she stopped in one corner. While others were making room for her to pass, she bent down and searched on the floor, touching every tile. A few seconds later she pushed into the floor. The floor started to separate underneath her hands and revealed a secret passage. Quickly, she motioned everyone to go down with the stairs. It was dark beneath but when she held her hand above the entrance, light streamed down. While the soldiers were making plans to break down the door, Ishtar managed to get everyone down the stairs. "Stay here, I will soon light up the passage for you to walk through", she yelled and closed it again by pressing on the opening stones. Just then, the door was yanked open and the soldiers pushed the furniture out of the way. "I can't believe you idiots forgot to carry explosives! Why are you soldiers if you are not prepared at all times?" the chief was shouting at the door. Ishtar had no time to think. Next thing she knew was that her feet were running through the wall. She was still holding the blanket and immediately covered herself when she got into the next room. The soldiers just managed to enter the other room then. They were all shocked to find no one inside. "But…but I saw a lot of people running into this room." One said to the others. "Yes, yes me too." They confirmed. Their chief came in and yelled orders. "Fools, we all know that they came in here. Look around for signs of another door or passage. They can't escape. This group carries the answer to every single mission we missed." That was the cue for Ishtar to start running again. She removed the blanket. "There is light again in the other room!" a soldier screamed again. Ishtar ran as the others were approaching. She pushed the first soldiers with so much forced out of the way and ran passed them. As they were grabbling to regain balance she went through the kitchen and out the back door. She aimed for the gate as the soldiers were catching up behind her. Just as the first one was reaching out to catch her, she jumped high. Every time she jumped, her feet would be above the soldier's heads and land again. She continued running. Then the old lady's voice came through to her. "We can see you, child. We know what you can do. It's time that you believe in yourself." While running, Ishtar closed her eyes for a second and leaped into the sky. This time she started to fly. There was doubt in the mind and she could not go higher. She went up and down, struggling like a beginner, while the soldiers were trying to grab her feet. The chief of the soldiers ran to his car when he saw her abilities. He reached behind his seat and took out a device that resembled a bomb. It was having two switches, blue and red. He screamed to his man to cover their faces with the masks they had attached to their belts. Then he pressed the blue switch. Strong rays with a heavy vibration came from the device and quickly covered the area. As it streamed towards Ishtar, with the next jump, the rays struck her and she disappeared. Then the chief soldier switched off the device smiling. "Well, I could never. It seems as if our leaders are truly prepared." He said while looking at the small device that held so much power. "Go in and search the entire house. We must find the others." They went in and searched everywhere but could find no one. What they didn't realize was that Ishtar was above the protective cloud which was created by the rays of the device. To the unwise eye, the explosion was just that. But in fact it was a device which releases energy that covers the entire place up to 12km in a bubble. This was designed to keep out forces from other places and planets and weaken the energies of those gifted inside the bubble. The chief soldier didn't know its use and seemingly the powers associated with it. He simply followed instructions. But he was supposed to use the device when they got to the house not after. Now, the others were underground and untouchable while Ishtar was in the air and just pushed to higher altitude. They were all out of harm's way. While she was floating unseen in the air, the soldiers started retreating. The chief rushed over to his house. He woke up his wife and son. "It is time, we move out." Is all he said to his family. Trained by years of being with him, the other two immediately got their belongings and rushed to the car. The chief went inside the kitchen and opened a drawer and took out a phone and remote control. He dialed a number and gave a report of everything that transpired that night. The receiver listened without interruption. When the soldier finished the person on the other side simply said. "Destroy". As the convoy of soldiers were starting to drive out of the area and soon reach the outskirts of the town, the chief pressed the remote. Immediately the town was in dust and flames. In the room where the receiver of the call was, a light turned green on his large computer screen. Showing two thirds of towns on the map marked green. He knew that another city and its people were gone. However, he was not happy. It was the first time that they encountered one with light as a force. Yes, the strangers helping the earthlings had powers of note.

Unexplainable supernatural powers. Yet, never in history was there one with light. Light, either from the dress she was wearing or some other source. He was glad that they destroyed them all but it would have been good if the light bearer was captured. He decided not to inform the others of this light bearer until he has sufficient information about its source. It was time to visit the oracle once more. Unknown to them, beyond the skies, movement started. Ishtar's body was rejuvenated by the stars as she floated above in the sky. She was becoming one with them as her glow was increasing. When she opened her eyes, she decent once more to the place that was now lying in ruins. On her way to the side where the house was, she found three children hurdled under a pile of bricks, crying. They were dark skinned with pure blonde hair and blue eyes. She reached out to them and they all went together to the place where the others were hiding and waiting; the very spot where she first knelt to press on the floor and came to a standstill. This time it opened by itself. They entered and she lit up the tunnel with her presence and everyone started walking. No one asked of the destination. No one questioned the events that just unfold. They all just knew that they were heading to safety and that was enough. That night, Ishtar slept in the underground tunnels with the others.

CHAPTER NINE

Earlier morning, she met with the elderly lady to discuss her plan. To her surprise, the other informed her that she doesn't need an explanation from Ishtar. Her task for now was simply to open the portal that had to lead them out of the city but that the two leading ladies knew just how to lead them to their destination from the tunnels. She touched Ishtar's head and asked her to close her eyes. Seconds later, Ishtar was back in the Capital city and it was a special day. It was the 21st of March 2020; the day that Ishtar turned 30 together with the host country. All around her people were busy with preparations of the country's birthday celebrations. Forgotten was the war waging all around the world and the immediate danger in towns closer to the city. Forgotten was the plight of the hungry, the need for water and all life giving necessities. The government availed millions to decorate the streets and prepare a gathering which was to see dignitaries from other countries coming to play with the governors of the country. This was the only little time during the past years that she didn't feel alone. The gods had indeed favoured her. It was a cunny trick of their s to send her to earth on such a special day. Twenty first March, marked the entrance of Saturn into Aquarius. This movement had the power to loosen boundaries in the universe and the energies worked together to lightened the responsibilities of earthlings. This and many astrological evidence made Ishtar aware that she was not alone in the battle to free the people of Alkebulan. She could sense that the 21st March, 30 years celebrations of her life on earth was about to turn different. The many questions she had would be answered on that day. Yes, there were instances over the short period of time were she was shown that she was unique and not from this world. The things she did, the dreams she felt, were all not in line with the ways of the people of Alkebulan. There were some she could related with but they would show only a glimpse of what they could do. When she asked them questions they would disappear.

The country's president called for a special gathering. Though millions of atrocities were taking place all around, he was certain that it would be the turning point for his government. He broadcasted nationwide that a huge festival would be held outside the capital city in the open plain just 30km away. This would allow many people access to the celebration. Busses and trains were engaged to travel people from far and wide. Food and drinks were made available in abundance and music groups came from all corners of the country. There was only one requirement from the Office of the President that day, that everyone wear white clothes. This was to mark the beginning of a new decade, to re-establish peace and inform the people that the government found new ways for economic freedom. Ishtar was excited. For some time now, she could sense that things were either going to change for the better or worse. She knew that her time has matured to move over to warfare. When she heard the message from the President over the radio, her heart skipped and sadness covered her body temple. Like many light workers all around the galaxies, she knew that economic freedom would come at a huge cost for the people of Alkebulan. Blood may flow again and the devastation now experienced would be nothing in comparison of what was to come. She shivered at the thought of all that lay ahead all the while, she knew that Alkebulan was not ready for what laid ahead. When the hour of the celebrations was upon them, her heart started beating irregularly. She was sweating and short of breath. Knowing that these were signs telling her to stay away from the celebrations. Ishtar was afraid. It was the first time that her body temple revolted against any of her movements. With certainty, she knew that what was to come was either to hurt her or the people of the country and world at large. Likewise she knew that she could not stay away. At 6am that morning, she prepared herself and left the little storehouse which she had turned into accommodation. Dressed in an exquisite white dress without shoes, she walked down the streets. Everyone was in a merry state of mind. The streets were bursting with people all moving and driving in the same direction. Within a few minutes the city was abandoned. Ishtar decided to walk the 30 kilometers to the venue, that way she could see how people were deserting the busiest city in the country. She walked passed many houses where there was no sign of life, not even dogs barking. From the backstreets of the less fortunate to the suburbs she walked. At the border of the two suburbs was a cemetery that was built on a large acre of land with a boundary wall that covered the entire stretch. It was a matter of either jumping the wall for a short cut or walking along the long boundary wall to get to the other side. As this was a usual trend by many she decided to jump into the cemetery. As she was walking briskly across the cemetery the wind started blowing softly. This was a special wind for it was carrying a message for Ishtar. As the wind passed her ears, she could hear voices. She looked around but could see no one. Her first thought was to run but then she slowed down her movement and listened to the voices. In the beginning it came through in hissing form but as she became more attentive she could hear the melody. A soft melody that soothed her heart and mind. It stayed with her until she reached the gate on the other side of the cemetery. At the gate stood an ancient woman, dressed as a shaman. She was tall and fierce in structure but her eyes were soft. Holding a tiny necklace in her hand. Ishtar approached her with caution drawn by the power of the friendly eyes. When she finally reached her they stood for some minutes watching each other in silence. Then the woman bends down and put the necklace around Ishtar's neck. She then touched her head reassuringly and opened the gate for Ishtar. Ishtar knew that this was a spirit from the seven seas because she could not communicate with her. Those from the sea had a different way of communicating with earthlings and Ishtar was not yet initiated for it, but it was reassuring to know that they were there. She was afraid yes, for the world was larger and populated more than any planet. The gods didn't reveal yet how she was to plan her fight to free the people. From every human and celestial experiences all she could gather was the affirmation that she was the chosen one to rescue the people. The how was hidden from her mind. On this day therefore was the first day of reassurance that she was not alone. At that moment she gathered courage and walked out the gate. She proceeded through the empty streets of the urban houses and joined the main road leading out of the city. As she was walking, two busses which were late rushed by and stopped at various intervals but she refused to get on. The passengers waved at her singing independence songs and while the busses were driving off into the distance. Suddenly, there was a loud sound in the sky and she saw fighter jets flying past. Her heart skipped for a moment. However, immediately they started releasing smoke in different colours and she smiled. Ishtar murmured softly to herself. "Not yet dear, not yet. You will know when the time would strike. She stood still in her tracks and watched the sky. It was beautiful, the colours were in different forms, painting all sorts of happy signs. Earthlings knew how to celebrate and show their happiness. She wondered for a brief moment why they couldn't just remain happy. The same way they are joining today would have been the perfect peaceful lifestyle hope for. Shaking her head at the thoughts she was about to walk on when something else caught her eye. A differently shaped phone arrived amongst the jets. She immediately identified the triangle shape belonging to Andromeda. Andromeda was inhabited by the giants of the galaxy. A first breed by the gods. In an attempt to create humans, they were fused between a cross of animal and people. They had great powers to align the galaxy but lacked the one source to access Earth. In their times they concurred the other planets to bow to their government and struggled for years to access the plains of Planet C-53. They were jealous that the smaller in stature beings on earth had the power they lacked to move between the soil and all other realms. They could not stand the fact that they had no access to the champers of the gods, let alone visitation rights to Planet C-53 to breathe the same air they were breathing. This was until the earthlings started messing up the planet's atmosphere. With a leakage in the ozone layer that separated them from space beings, they created a portal for other beings to enter. Over the last century, life from outer space entered Planet C-53 through that portal but time and again, they were overpowered by the people of Alkebulan and returned to their respective planets. This time however, the giants decided to come in person. Ishtar knew that their presence could not spell any good for the host planet. She started running into the field, off the main road searching for an open space with a flat surface from which she could make contact with the ship. After 30minutes of frantic search, she found the desired space. Breathless she stood in the open while exposing every cell of her being to the sky above. Ishtar was aware that the giants from Andromeda had no gentle string in their hearts and she was a weakling caged in the body temple. She didn't know what to expect. Yet, with everything within her, she lit up. Slowly, the golden glow emanating from her body lit up her surroundings too. She knew this was a big risk but the need to know why they were here being more important. One thing was assuring; that they could only hurt the body temple but not kill it for the golden fence was securing her safety. The leader of the ship saw the golden light and steered the ship in that direction. Their identifiers could not place the being that stood in the middle of the glowing circle. As they ascended, they could sense the strong forces surrounding it. The energies were too strong and the closer their ship tried to get to the surface of the earth, it was shaken out of position. The leader screamed orders to his crew to prepare for war in case the being below proved dangerous. He was worried. Their research and observations of Planet C-53 never showed presence of such power. They knew that some selected beings carried celestial powers but never to this extend. After some time of trying to land the ship, the leader stopped trying and decide to communicate to the being. He introduced himself and asked for permission to enter the golden space. Ishtar granted him the privilege through an eliminated golden light, set up like a ladder from their ship to the feet of Ishtar. The leader and several of his men ascended to meet the force below. As they reached the soil, the veil upon the body temple of Ishtar was lifted and they recognized her. Immediately they fell on their knees. "Hail to you goddess Ishtar, may we find favour in your sight." They sang in union. "Hail to you mighty ones from D66. What brings you here?" she asked. "My Queen, in fairness of our noble deeds thus far pardon us. We are not here to war against the earthlings.   By the observations of the houses of governors in the galaxy we feared that the ongoing distractive measures of the human race was soon going to destroy the entire universe. After consultations with all governing bodies of the great Andromeda a decision was made to give the being of Planet C-53 an ultimatum. This is why we are here." The leader answered. "I bow to you great leader of the skies above. Speak to me the ultimatum as I stand to represent that which is beyond you and the skies."

"My Queen, we lay bare our humble existence for we were not aware that the House of the Lords, greater and beyond has favoured the human race that much to appear in person to reprimand its creation. We thought as the gods are silent and their ancestors turned their backs on them we would set them straight."

"We take note of your concern, great and mighty one but return to your space until such time that a call is send for you to sweep the skies clean. This is not yet the time for the earthlings did not have enough time to prove themselves worthy of the space granted to them." With great resign the aliens retracted and left Planet C-53 as swiftly as they arrived. Ishtar fell to the ground exhausted. She has never used so much power before and knew it was going to take tremendous time before she could regain all her powers. Her walk to the independence celebrations was cut short as she lay in the dust. Perhaps she was meant to walk the path only to meet the two beings she did.

Sometime later, Ishtar woke up in a meadow surrounded by exotic plants and lush trees. She looked around in confusion to see what may have happened to the people she was leading. The scenery in front was completely different from the one where she was the night before. She balled her fist in frustration and beat hard on the ground where she was lying and spoke to herself. "This had to stop. For how long was she going to disappear and reappear at strange places without finding a complete answer of what was happening? By now it was clear that she was to save the world. But how was she going to accomplish that if there were forces beyond her dragging her all over the place." Looking around this new environment was sort of bringing peace to her soul. She could sense that all her answers were possibly hidden in this beautiful valley. A few steps away from her eleven women were sitting in a circle and singing. When they saw that she was regaining consciousness, one of them came and led her to their side. They let her sit amongst them and continued singing. As their voices rose so did the leaves of the trees. The winds were quiet and though she could see the presence of birds and other animals, she could hear no other sound except the singing. It was quiet. Through the singing voices she could experience nature around her. It had an expectant aura in itself. As if something mayor was due to happen. She waited with the silent air around her. Not understanding yet again what she was doing. Yet waiting. When they finished singing the women knelt in a silent prayer which lasted for ten minutes. While the others were still kneeling the one that brought Ishtar signaled to her to follow her as she was standing up. As they started walking away, Ishtar turned to see that the other women also stood up and went their way.

"We are the Medicanice. The gatekeepers of Lula. The great mother goddess of Timba our land. We are warriors guarding the seven cities of Lula against intruders." She said as if responding to a question. She looked in Ishtar's confused eyes and smiled. "You shall not understand today but you are safe. You were brought here to allow time to remove the shades from your eye. This will allow you to see why you were sent to us and many that need your help."

"How could I possibly be off help to anyone?" Ishtar asked. "All I ever do is strange things that scare me as I disappear or appear at will like a magician in different places."

"Yes, indeed you are confused." The woman replied with a chuckle. "I am Sofia, the Chief Priestess and combat instructor. I will soon introduce you to the other light workers. For now please do not worry. Let me show you to your resting quarters. By night fall, I will come again and we will dine. Soon everything will be cleared."

Early the next morning, Sofia opened Ishtar's door and entered the room without raising noise. She stood silently at Ishtar's bedside, only her aura was enough to wake the other from her sleep. Ishtar enjoyed the presence and calm spirit of Sofia and lingered a bit longer in bed with closed eyes. Upon this Sofia chuckled and touched her to stand up. "Wake up our Queen, I know you are simply enjoying the peace but we have limited time and a lot to cover." Ishtar smiled and stretched herself to full length in bed. "Aah so you knew all along who I was? She asked the lady smiling. "No my Queen we didn't. Though we were prepared to receive a guest for training. The mirror all seeing was blocked and we did not know. At midnight the great presence of Amma served us a visit. A visit which didn't occur over the past hundred thousand years. My Queen, the mysteries of the gods we may not understand all the time. Just as we don't understand now what we could possible teach one of the creators of our being." Ishtar rose from the bed and the priestess bowed to the ground immediately in respect. "No don't do that wise one. You are the eyes of the gods but in their wisdom they saw it fit that the body temple I have borrowed should be subjected to all human feelings. I had to be them to understand how best to serve them. Yes, I am able to sweep them off the planet in one breath as we are not to feel and reason like you. But in the eyes of the great Amma, your race is special. I'm therefore caged in this body temple, stripped from almost all powers to find the best way to be of assistance to you all. Please stand up Wise One, let the eye of the gods not bow towards the sand. Stand tall as the gods have deemed you worthy to stand in equality with them in the world." "Ase" Sofia bowed while confirming the blessing. Then she started to prepare a bath for Ishtar. After bathing they had breakfast with the other priestesses in the garden. "Here we only eat live giving food, your body may resist it for a couple of days as our human race is consuming the wrong substances that doesn't aid their bodies. The type of food they eat and the amounts of sugar intake harms their body. Hence the many illnesses it has created. Though nature has its own share, humans are the sole creators of the deadliest illnesses which are occurring in their world. Thus, for the following ten days your body will be re-introduced to the right way of eating." Sofia informed her.

It was a painful experience as Ishtar was greeted by diarrhea that night. She has never experienced such level of intense pain. Her stomach felt as if it was curled up in a knot and fighting spirits within. She was vomiting and releasing toxic elements from her body all night long. With agony, sweat and a light fever, she battled through the first three nights. To keep her hydrated, Sofia brought her the sweetest water from one of the choice fountains in the garden. Explaining that her body had to wash out all toxic and renew her taste buds. In between the pains and crawling on the cold floor for some relieve, Ishtar would laugh at the thought of the beings she needs to guide. "Why would they subject their own bodies to such level of pain and torture by eating garbage instead of eating the correct way?" She looked up to the roof in projection of it as the sky above and shook her head. "Amma, the Supreme Creator. I don't think I understand the complexities of this species you so love dearly." After the cleansing ritual she realized that although her body mass dropped she was feeling more energized and walked around more stable than before. Her body felt renewed. That day they celebrated the end of her food treatment with exotic fruits, one bite into a strange looking berry flipped her mind back to the time she spend with Oracle Mable. The priestess was telepathic and held her hand tight. "Not now" she said gently. "Focus please. The time for you to have access to all worlds has not come yet." Though she didn't understand the meaning of it all Ishtar could do was knot her head in agreement.

She was then introduced to the other ten priestesses who were all around them in silence from the day she came. Alkebulan in its modern condition had 54 independent states. Though not all could be represented by the Medicanice, those from the largest or most influential states were selected for the mission. Access to all other priestesses worldwide was not denied and their absence was confirmed in positive light.

From Cairo, Bastet the protector, the priestess of music, children, arts and warfare to Isis, the priestess of motherhood and fertility from Khartoum. As the introductions continued Ishtar realized why they were specially selected. They were to aid her untrained body into the perfect ways of human combat. The streets of Johannesburg and its surroundings brought forth Mamlambo, Aicha Kandisha from the budding Casablanca, Yemaya from the mighty Lagos, from the plains of Nairobi, Olapa, the "White Lady of Tassili 'n Ajjer, from Ras ben Sakka, Tanith and Calypso from the seas of Cape Algulhas. Under their guidance, Ishtar was taught how to fight in both realms and space against the forces of darkness which was behind the destruction of Alkebulan. She also learned the gentle acts of love they freely shared in both realms.

Part of Ishtar's training involved understanding of Alkebulan's wild life. During ancient times, animals and humans were sharing the same space including language and mind. They helped each other in building their habitat into the dynasty it has become. They fought wars together and also knew how to cultivate its resources for the common good of every living being. The images she saw in her dreams about the beautiful paradise of Oracle Mable was to become a true living sensation for her in this part of her existence. She was to leave the village of the priestesses and join the plant and animal kingdom with only Sofia as her escort. But before the journey she was to be conditioned that night, the goddesses brought coloured and perfumed water to her cabin. For the first time, they actually touched her by washing her entire body in the reddish water. She was accustomed to the !Nau* powder used by the women of Namibia as part of their beauty treatment. The washing in a similar coloured water was a new thing though. As usual, she didn't ask questions. In any case there was no need as the priestesses would explain everything they did through song and chants. All that was required was for her to sit silently and listen to them sing. It all became clear very soon through the song. For the trees and beast of the Animal kingdom to identify with her, she was to smell different. The modern human scent was repulsive to them and would have them jump out of their gentle state into dangerous warrior beings. It was thus important for them to get to know her slowly and the red perfumed water was to help in tricking them. After bathing she was covered in a brown animal skin and one of the ladies brought a hot spicy drink for her to drink before going to bed.

The next morning Ishtar left before the sunrise with Sofia. They walked far and wide. Crossing various fields, rivers and valleys. At one point during the walk, Ishtar fell on the ground with exhaustion. Sofia just looked at her and laughed, explaining that they haven't even reach the middle of their destination. To her, this proved that Ishtar was definitely not ready as they have foretold. She would need the powers hidden in the secret gardens of the Animal Kingdom to make her conquest easier. With a click of the tongue, she reprimanded Ishtar.

"Queen of the greater skies. Your chosen vessel for the journey ahead was a wise chose but you are not utilizing it to its full potential. The body temple housing you is of great importance for one to travel with speed and accuracy to reach the desired destination. From the nomadic San people, you have gained body and blood streams that can navigate routes as they are excellent trackers, further their ability to reserve energy and water levels through the type of foods they ate. You will have the ability to walk for miles on end. Determination is the catch phrase for the Nama people thus you could make use of all these elements to ignite your powers.

She met them all at one interval. Grootslang was a monster that lived in a cave called Wonder Hole in the Richtersveld. His powers were so great that the gods subdivided it into two species in modern Africa which were the elephant and snake. However, Ishtar was to meet the original species in this part of the world. Inkanyamba was a huge eel-like animal that could control the weather. Kongamato a flying monster living in rivers and swamps but one without feathers. Then there was the lightning bird known as the Impundulu with powers of a shape shifter, its eggs were used for medicinal powers. From the Ewe people, Adze the vampire with the form of a firefly, could revert into human appearance. In its normal form, it sucked blood and spread diseases. Bili Ape was a large chimpanzee that behaved like a large gorilla. Gbahali resembled a crocodile and grew thirty feet long. He joined them from the rivers of Ghana. Ninki Nanka; a dragon like creature with the body of a crocodile, head of a horse with horns and a long neck like a giraffe was also representing the animal kingdom together with Popabawa a demon who appeared as a normal human being by day and a one eyed, bat winged monster at night. They were mostly found alongside the spice region of Zanzibar. The cryptic resembling a dinosaur called Mokèlé-mbèmbé came from the region of Congo and lastly the Tikoloshe a gremlin who was send by a shaman to vex his enemies. That was the line up from the animal kingdom to assist Ishtar together with the iconic trees of Alkebulan which were the Fever, Baobab, Sausage, Quiver, Leadwood, Marula, Whistling Thorn, Mopane, Sycamore Fig and the Dragon blood. At the end of three excruciating weeks Ishtar was returned back in the care of Sofia. She took her to the most exclusive side of the village. To the eye of Ishtar, this was the most captivating location she has escaped too. Covered with lush trees and various flowers she found herself in a little paradise. Small rivers were flowing around in harmony with the sound of birds and other creatures. Although it was quite to the normal ear. The alleviated beings could hear the musical vibrations. Sofia knew immediately that this was one area where she didn't need to explain anything to Ishtar. Her spirit lit up by the recognition of the vibrations all around them. She was able to project her mind to the beta state at the sound of the meditative sounds. No one could explain to a goddess how to feel at one in her own space. Thus, she slowly turned back and left. The state of Ishtar's being entirely transformed in the valley. Her outer eyes closed, as the spirit eye was opening to connect with the one world she knew better than anything. She started walking blindly until she reached a cliff. There, her spirit sat waiting. After a while, she felt the presence of Amma siting silently next to her. She felt at home. Reassured and strengthened mentally. She sat there smiling. Then as she was returning, she heard Amma speak. "It is well."

She returned to the location of the priestesses and as they looked at her in total surprise for she was gone for forty days, Ishtar smiled, for it was just a blink of an eye in her world. To her spirit being, she was gone for but a brief moment. Tomorrow awaited the final journey to lead the people of Alkebulan.

CHAPTER TEN

Everyone wanted to have a piece of the pie. After all, it was their world. In the beginning of times, they were given dominion over the earth. It was theirs to manage. The Master Creator had perfect plans for the species called men. Though they were not the only species in the universe, within them, they carried a different view of the world. Minds governed by a misconception so great; one named entitlement and the other selfish greed. Oh, the souls just knew how to create things for their comfort and live well. Yet, hidden deep within them was aggressiveness which boiled like a silent volcano the sight of hiddenness which threaten their comfort. They would lash out in a destructive manner. In the name of national security, they would war against each other. Kill, burn, bomb and erase their own from the face of the world. What went wrong, Ishtar wonder? According to the books of life, humans are the exalted species because they gained favour from the gods from all galaxies. They are referred with high regard and feared and envied simultaneously. They have the divine power of choice which lacks from all other species and have free access to two different plains, moving swiftly between realms of note, yet lacking the understanding to be great as a united front. Their capacity of learning is extraordinary, as they have the power to conquer each other's' languages and evolve into multi-lingua, multi-cultured beings. The power of choice has coloured their world in many wonderful ways; making them creators of various things. Everything that is on Earth, both in human and animal kingdoms is wired differently. They are the only species to mate and reproduce their own offspring. While others in different galaxies are presented with their packages on the front porch. They have the privilege of reincarnating into a body temple and progress through babe to adult stages. A body temple which is one of the best piece of architecture which is a powerful link that connects both body and soul. Yes, incarnation is possible for many species but divine benefit for the exalted spirits which a chosen for Earthly mission is the body temple as an exclusive choice; living space that can recreate, transform and grow. A type of source not available in other spaces of live. These divine creators have not just dominion, they are the only beings who possess powers so great to whom the makers of the Earth bows as they created them with so much love and given them rights denied to others. These rights which prohibit the creators from ownership. These earthlings are Kings and Queens in their own right with access to grace both worlds with ease. They have the power to reign on Earth and in Heaven; that has been the great commission during inception. However, something sacred and horrific at the same time must have occurred during the production stages which may have blinded the third eye. The exalted beings had no clue, whatsoever to live in a perfect world they received on a platter.

Today as she walks or jumps and runs with uncertainty through one experience to another, Ishtar picks up a thought or two. Humans needed help. Though she knew without doubt that she was assigned to the rescue team, what was starring her in the face was the question of how to help a self-destructive being. Instead of expanding into greatness, they were the only species living backwards. They were destroying the livelong blessing of the body temple by unhealthy lifestyles, which made it vulnerable and prone to diseases. The abundance in food choices which was poisonous to the body temple, hygiene and self-care that was applied wrongly, neighbourly love which was misplaced. Such was the order of the supposedly great people and animals of Mother Earth. None of them had the wisdom to remove the blinds to connect the dots. Their living pattern reduced to one of birth, eating, growing, reproduction and death and on the technological and scientific fields, being the species designated to a piece of empty dirt, they had a powerful artistry and sense to create a dynasty. A paradise that grew into perfection from nothing. Making them one entity which was not spoon fed but left to evolve on their own terms. Their curiosity to evolve was meant to be the driving force. Unfortunately, they are the very beings breaking down the kingdoms they have created. Ishtar has learned that the beings called Earthlings or people don't need enemies from elsewhere. They are their own enemies and very destructive as well. They build and admire each other's works, yet, turn around and pull each other apart. Today unfortunately they have brought themselves to their knees and the continent of Alkebulan which was the birth place of all divine. The gateway to evolution has been reduced to nothing. Mother Earth setting tears so painful, while looking on how her beloveds are destroying each other and the only source of life they possess. It is because the soil objected and called out for rescue that Ishtar was sent. As Mother Earth's sobbing became louder under the vibrations of other energies, her message was received in codes. None of the receiving beings in other galaxies could interpret it fully. Only the house of the Divine Priestess could make out some sense of it. They sensed that Mother Earth was not able to send her babies into the bottomless pit of hell fire. She wanted them rescued. She wanted a second chance which would allow them to go through atonement and heal in order to path a way to rebuild what they have broken. To Ishtar, this was a simple, sorry case of a spoiled child and over protective mother. Yet, she could not refuse when the despair call came through. And so did many over the centuries. There has been one rescue mission after the other. Through these experiences, each rescuer that returned would report that this was the most arrogant species alive. Yet time and again they would rise in support of Mother Earth to rescue her offspring. As she walks through yet another ghost town while looking at what could be and what has remained, Ishtar realizes that they were leading this rescue mission wrong. This species didn't need more wars and destruction. They were not designed to be ruled. They were to govern themselves with the understanding of love to keep them united. Now, Ishtar was getting the understanding that she was to lead them to a new place to re-start their lives and re-create a new paradise. She was to lead them on a golden trail to discover the city of gold. Ishtar looked deep within to leap yet into another sphere. She had to meet the people in the safe haven of the light workers.

Ishtar rose from the ground and looked at the millions of souls people sited all around the cliff. This is but a small amount of those remaining in some parts of the world. Many were dying of wars, diseases, natural disasters, hunger, pollution and other challenges. However, the biggest killers that burn out the human race was by their own hands. They overestimated the power of greed. They didn't understand that their power was to serve a greater purpose. One of unity and not division, just as it is in the realms above. Humans didn't need a ruler as the observance of natural principals was enough but due to the nature of their disobedience, one was elected each time during different seasons to keep them intact. They were indeed the favourite species of Amma. While holding on to the pleasures of both worlds, they were destined for greatness, a collective greatness. In its single entity, it could never work. Ishtar slowly stretched out her hands to draw everyone's attention. For the first time in her existence now and beyond, she bowed to the people of Alkebulan.

"My people, I greet you. Looking at you all around. I see beautiful, happy faces. Faces that have withstood many storms to get here. You of Alkebulan have overcome many obstacles and remain standing but I ask myself today. For how long? You have it all, or so you may think. In your quest to race against time, did you see what you have done? The moon is bleak. The sunrise not so happy anymore. There is blood on your hands; that of many of your brothers. And what was the gain thereof. Alkebulan was once great because it was not divided by greed, colour and leaders. It was great because it understood the power of love. With all it animals, wild and tame, the seasons colourful and the rivers flowing, there was the understanding that you are a sacred being. Given the godly power of procreation and access to all the wisdom shared through Solomon, you were to manage the piece of soil for progression of the world and other sister planets. I shed a tear today for my soul can't celebrate at the thought of handing back the reigns of this kingdom in your slippery hands. Over decades, the gods have send their sons and daughters every single time you erred. Not because the gods are not wise, this recurrence was simply because of that one unseen force that binds us together. The force called first love. You are loved, you were loved and you shall be loved. However, every parent needs a time when they have to cut the umbilical cord. Though I fear for another angel to come to wage your wars, or Amma himself to ascend in fury to rebuild or possibly destroy you for good, I am confident that you have the power to rise and rebuild yourself for the better. Alkebulan, understand that you are the beginning of the human race. You always have been. From your loins, every other being came to life. For there was only one world before the beginning of your many countries. Its parent and creator the androgynous and omnipresent. The one source above any other. There was no division as the flat grounds upon which you are sitting was one. Your children came in all shades of colour, only separated by the tides of your climate. None foreign to the other as the identity that serves within the body temple is one. This is the ultimate knowledge which was to be stored in your mind and not what was hidden in the House of Truth, for that which was locked under secret doors was not from Amma. You need to learn to cultivate and align your energies correctly. See, when the wars break out or disasters strike, you always come together as one formidable force to heal the world, your home. During that one time, you forget that you spoke in different dialects or didn't eat the same food or wear the same cultures on your sleeves. You simply obey the unspoken code of cameradie, the patriotic urge to stand together for the good of the world was speaking much louder than anything and you pushed against the thread. Yes, unfortunately many transitioned during such trying times but time and again you rise. Alkebulan is blood stained and carries heavy under the load of guilt for allowing her child to run wild. It is time to return to your senses and clean your house. Let the warriors rise to safeguard the boarders of Alkebulan again, the priestesses and mighty oracles rise to provide guidance required just like before, the children learn the wisdoms buried in the bosoms of Alkebulan, the men rise and take up responsibility and kingship and let the kingdoms, both human, plant and animal unite to peaceful existence. Time after time you release power to strengthen and heal. Now is the time to do it again."

While Memnon was gathering his subjects for the greatest war of them all; a war which would mark the end of times not only for the people of Alkebulan but any other who didn't align with him, Ishtar's training came to an end. After thirty good years she was one with herself. She could feel all the emotions flooding through her body temple, recognized why it was sacred and also understood the need for it to house the living spirit of Amma. They were one. As the creator is, so its product. That which has fallen off the bandwagon by choice had no reason to live. There was no reason to be pitiful. Those behind the destruction of

Alkebulan had no plan whatsoever to spear the great people of Amma. It was time to reconcile the fact that was eminent. Only through the fierce tunnel of war, she was to free the people. In the current atmosphere clouded by fear, their minds were not in one place. This is why she was here to gather them and show them how to get to a place of ultimate peace. Before peace though, liberation, be it through the barrel of the gun or celestial powers, Ishtar returned to Windhoek. She has been all over the country avoiding the one place which was at the center of all the hype. Windhoek was not only the capital city of Namibia. It was also the place of hot springs and the four wind corners. While it served as the hiding place for Memnon's headquarters, it was the ideal place to start warfare. She could have the power of earth, wind, fire and air all in one place to execute her plan to destroy Memnon. She was in the highlands from where she could observe the movement of Memnon and his subjects. Their headquarters were at the Heroes Acre. A well disguised space as it stood for the commemoration of fallen war veterans of the country. Strategically placed a few miles away from the city's hustle and bustle. Firstly, no one in the world would have ever thought of a place in a developing country to search for the most powerful man on earth. Secondly, the monument and space was exclusive; well-guarded and only accessible to the public at prescribed hours. As the citizens of the country lost trust in their leaders and rejected all that they represented, this space became a white elephant. Only visited by tourists and well-wishers with money. For the rest of the population, it was simply another place where leaders spent government funds which could have been used elsewhere to bury each other. As the traffic to and fro the Heroes Acre was not much, it was an ideal hide out. Built with the modern technologies, the underground access was utilized for another reason. No one knew of Memnon's operations under the surface of the Acre. Not even the secret service of the country and its president.

They were given better toys to play with while operations proceeded unseen. At the hands were discussions of how to gather their wealth, they knew that it was just a matter of time before all their loan sharks from other governments were going to close up on them. The Chinese already took over the mines, airport and harbor. The Americans refused to print their money and placed sanctions on everything that was Alkebulan, not only Namibia. The friendships they deposited on turned their heads away. Money deposited in its billions in banks abroad was no longer traceable. They were cornered and the forecast was slavery back in the hands of those from whom they thought they were liberated. Unfortunately, their eyes could not see far. Hence, they didn't know that the world all-around has been under the same attack. The economies all around were broken down. The supply chain of wealth and power broken. The people were defeated and amidst such chaos, no one had time to consider protecting the borders because the unseen enemy was fighting a different type of war. Due to the virus released, humans self-destructed. Instead of standing as a united front, people were scared of each other. They were constantly tortured by thoughts of suicide. The system tried to isolate everyone in a bit to drive them to insanity or suicide as the virus manipulated their minds to act in that manner but the people realized that the only way to beat the manipulation was to remain together. They hid from the unseen enemy and kept together. Ishtar's task was to seek out the safe houses were the people gathered and lead them on a secret trail. During her first exposures thereof, she didn't understand what was required. However, as time passed, she just acted on impulse. Wherever she encountered people, she would simply glow and light up a path for them as her intuition decreed. She no longer asked why and how but just acted at will. Memnon discovered that the person his Chief Security Officer described six months ago when he placed a call through from Okahandja was the source to lead him to the final key. He knew that she was the keeper of the secret which would open the treasures of gold written in the scrolls. However, she proved to have celestial powers which needed him to go out and track her down as his subjects wouldn't know how. Before that, he needed to open the chambers of his head office and dispatch the weapons of mass destruction they had hidden from the world. Ishtar watched and waited around for two days. When she saw movement by nightfall on the second day, she sat up prepared. Soldiers came out of a hidden exit on the south side of the Acre. The north was were the main gate and national security where roaming thus they made use of the south. The national security lingered around without any care. While the soldiers in black combat suits carried lights on the foreheads and ran in a straight file into the open field, they divided themselves in two rows and formed something that looked like a landing strip. Indeed, as Ishtar was watching a strange looking plane arrived and land right in the landing strip. Ishtar heighten her senses and focus her eyes on the plane. After the doors were opened, she saw Ben standing in there. Caught by surprise, she bent away for a minute and luckily just missed his gaze in her direction. Ben could sense the presence of another being but could not see any. When she regained composure, Ishtar lifted her body and repositioned herself. Her mind was going wild. It ran back in time. Painfully, she remembered the young man that came to the bridge and stayed with her and the other street children. He was gentle and helpful until the day he sold them out to a human trafficker. She came here led by her intuition to seek out Memnon. Right before her eyes stood Ben in all his glory. Was he the brains behind all these things she wondered? It made perfect sense. He knew how to manipulate others to believe everything he said. He had the power to read their thoughts and above all, he knew how to make things easier for them. Did he know that she was the chosen one then? She wondered. If so, why didn't he eliminate her back then? This and many other questions rushed through her mind while she was looking on how the soldiers were returning underground and erasing all their tracks. Ishtar didn't need to enter the place. The soldiers she saw were actually robots made at a manufacturing plant in China, a country trying for many years to clone humans. The past in everything except the challenge of getting the clone body structure to live and breathe by itself. Instead, they connect their mutations to the mainframe computers at the head office and charged them to life. With the high-tech sensory, they could operate like humans but lack emotions which was by default but perfect for the mission they had to execute. The developers were assassinated in China and Ben brought the specimens with him to Namibia. After the betrayal of his subjects all over the world, he chose to work with humanoid robots instead. He was certain that with the final codes in his possession he would be able to build a new world and a people according to his image and liking.

Ishtar had work to do and it needed an immediate start. She could not understand the reason behind Ben's presence at the headquarters of Memnon and it was time to check it out. She positioned herself on the ground at sat for 20 minutes in a meditative position. By channeling all her energies to one place, she was able to fix her root chakra with the soil beneath. In a spiral manner, her body was aligning itself with nature. For the human eye, the energies transporting to the ground beneath her would seem as if a root was leaving her body to penetrate the soil. As it being drilled, the roots were attaching the body and soil as one source. Through this energy transferal, Ishtar was gaining more power and her body temple filled with the needed source to support the spirit being within. After the connection has been made, Ishtar laid flat on the ground so that the energies can flow equally throughout her entire body temple. She reached a point of total oneness with nature; the source of the body temple and leap into an out of body experience. With all her consciousness bound to the body and through the root chakra the soil, she was able to leave the body and move the spirit to run across the open fields to the hidden door of Memnon's hide out. Her spirit entered through the walls and she drifted along the corridors. It was quite a sight to see advance architecture and showmanship which was employed beneath the ground. Memnon has set up an entire new structure beneath the actual Heroes Acre. There were three floors. The first floor consisted of all the modern 6G technology and its appliances which were utilised in the ongoing destruction of Alkebulan. There was weaponry which they never saw before but which was utilised such that people thought they were attacked by alien forces. Today, Ishtar saw that this were all works of Memnon, and not from the outer space. Though the aliens were equally advanced, she had their reassurance that they would not war against the humans. This agreement was already established during 30th the independence celebrations of Namibia, when she met them in the open fields west of Windhoek. Hence, there was no need to associate what she is witnessing today with them as they were bound by their words. Now, she could understand what type of equipment was used to blow up the industrial park where the Major of Okahandja was to host a meeting with his people and the subsequent destruction of the entire town. She could also now understand the reason behind all the 'ghost' towns she has seen across Alkebulan. The second floor was one giant science lab. There were many robotic men walking up and down, walking on various machinery and testing out chemicals. As she moved swiftly through the lab, she was drawn by a depression feeling. Following this feeling, she moved undetected between the robots to the far end of the floor. There, she was blocked by a glass door, which resembled a huge refrigerator. Inside it were cubicles containing bodies of Alkebulanians. As she moved between them while observing that they vary in age, size and body structure and all were women and some dating back as far as the Stone Age, she noticed that these bodies were used as guinea pigs for the laboratory experiments done. Outcomes thereof would then explain the outbreak of unknown epidemics in Alkebulan, the rest of the world and the swift appearance of antidotes once the required target of deaths has been achieved. Ishtar was gutted and as much as she wanted to destroy everything she saw; it was not possible these were all man made things and needed a body temple to destroy it. The spirit moving around this place only had access to the spirit world. She stopped abruptly as that source came to mind. Well, this was the reason why she needed to be in a human body. It became clear that she was not going to be able to fight the men without the consent from its hosts and with permission from Amma. With the excellence in creating human beings, Amma gave them the sole responsibility to govern themselves. Though they had his spirit dwelling in them, it was not by force but by a willing consent. Never could they interfere in earthly decisions unless granted permission thereof. Amma, gave them total dominion and though they had a responsibility towards serving him, he removed the right to impose upon them his ultimate will. This was his decision because he didn't want marionettes serving him as the outer space beings did. He wanted a race that could think and sustain itself provided they remain under law and principle. Many moons ago he continuously showed his power by punishing them in harsh ways when they didn't obey, but due to the cry of his angels, goddesses and ancestors, he made a vow never to interfere without permission and never to punish them with godly wrath. Ishtar now understood why her birth, related exposure in the human world and subsequent training was needed. Her powers had to align with the host body and just as they tuned in to execute this investigation, they needed to be one to complete the entire task that has before them. She continued to the last floor which was at the very deep bottom of the earth. The walls were all painted white and the light very bright. As her spirit moved forward, she realized that there was nothing on this floor. It was completely empty and void of all life. She looked around and wondered why they had to build a third floor if there was nothing to keep there. But just as she was wondering, a door opened at the right side from where she was standing. Instinctively, she moved closer to the wall and giggled within when she realized that she was a spirit thus could possibly not be seen and touched. Yet, she remained in a hidden position. Ben, followed by a few of his guards entered the floor and walked in her direction. As they were passing her, he stopped for a moment. Looked around, tried to stretch out his hands in all directions and stepped forward. He repeated that process a couple of times as he walked a few steps, then looked back and thought for a while. He then shook his head and proceeded to walk. Ishtar sighed with relief but realized then that Ben indeed may have some form of extra celestial powers. How else was he then able to sense that there was another presence in the place? Luckily, he couldn't be certain, hence he moved on. Ben and his entourage walked up to the center of the floor where he took out a small device from his pockets and pressed it. Immediately, a safe appeared in the center of the floor. He had his men open the big door of the safe and then he walked inside and came out with a scroll and while holding it up to the ceiling, he laughed and said. "This is the full script as given by the gods to our people, removed from the House of Truth. I was lucky enough to get away with the full manuscript while the other kings managed to steal partial copies of the original. Everything that we did this far and what lays beyond is all written in here. I have even managed to create more than what was stated in this scroll. However, it was one thing lacking. In the scroll there is a mention of a place of gold. The ultimate heaven promised for mankind. The place that here the mortals meet their creator. The place of abundance, where they are ruling in perfect alignment with the gods. It says to get to the place of gold, where riches and abundance abide, and one most follow the trail. There will be a source that leads the people on the trail to the place of gold it says. The world as it is, is no more. Now the time has come to find the gold trail and that source which is to lead the people of Alkebulan to its glory. With some of them destroyed and many under my manipulation, I will reign over the place of gold. I and only I will have total power. I will reign." The hollow floor echoed his words and vibrated under its weight. Ben took his time to re-read the scroll and there after replaced it in the volt. As he was replacing the scroll, Ishtar moved towards her exit. Her movement caused Ben to startle and he looked behind. Something was definitely in this place. He quickly closed the volt and rushed to his office on the first floor. There he instructed the guards to remain outside. He went inside and closed the door behind him. Then he rushed to another door and walked straight to his altar. He mumbled a few chants and sat in a kneeled position. Through the mirror before him, he saw Ishtar as she was standing up from the ground and running away from the place. Slowly he rose, with a satisfactory smile on his face. "Well, well" he sighed. "So my initial thoughts about this girl were right. I knew that she was special. For a chick that will grow into a cock can be spotted the very day it hatches. I knew that she was going to outsmart the human traffickers that's why I put her to test so that I could use her but she vanished. Her presence today simply means that she was joined the 'other side'. Yes, yes, I am aware that there a couple of priestesses fighting my subjects undercover. The only reason for her being here is that they might have trained her. I will need to follow her closely." He stayed with his eyes on Ishtar. She suddenly increased her speed and ran towards a big Baobab tree. A Baobab is an upside-down giant with a record-breaking lifespan, it is one of the continent's most iconic and outlandish trees. Its bark is fire resistant and they are extraordinary drought resistant. They are mostly found on the island of Madagascar and Ishtar had to travel all the way there to established trust with them to support the human course. Just like all the other plants and animals that agreed to stand in union with them, the Baobab tree agreed to be the escape route Ishtar needed to move from place to place.   As he was watching, she stretched out her hands and jump right into the base of the tree and disappeared. Ben was shocked and stumbled to the ground. "This is not possible, this cannot be", he screamed. "No this is not possible, I have destroyed the relationship between men and the plant and animal kingdom long ago. This is not possible, Noooooooooo! He screamed.

For nearly two days Ben kept himself under lock and key. He didn't eat anything; neither did he speak to anyone. His phone was ringing off the hook. The governors were worried as Ben called for an emergency meeting which was to take place in the next seven days. Just as it was done centuries ago, Ben was going to summon all the governors to one conference where he would reveal his true identity and kill them. They were coming to the meeting under the pretense of World Peace discussions. The World has passed through a great deal of torture over the past couple of decades and it was time to refocus and strategies. Hence the meeting which would separate the great from the chaff. Evidently, there was a lot of resistance. People were disappearing from the face of the earth and others were forging wars against the order. Thus, he knew that preparations were to be made. And he had it all under control. So far he outweighed every single thing the people were trying to do to save Alkebulan and he was prepared for it. What he wasn't aware of was that Alkebulan was not fighting alone. It came to realization that the world needed to be reunited. Though there was great distance between various continents and with the current global warming, many were still drifting apart under its current weight. Humans started recognizing the essence of life. Some evolved minds were increasingly teaching people the hidden secrets of quantum leaping and how to reunite the host body with its spirit. He had weapons build for that too and burned every single city that took part in such awakening rituals with its inhabitants. Only those cities were people chose not to think and act for themselves, remained. The last of the cities he thought was Okahandja when his Chief Security Officer reported to have spotted a glowing female being. Since then, there was no mention of any extra ordinary activities reported. He thought they had it all under control now. But what he saw two days ago disturbed him to the core. Yes, he knew that a source was to come forth to lead the people to the Promised Land. His first hunch is to track down Ishtar but true to his ancestry, only a fool tests the depth of a river with both feet. He will eat the elephant bit by bit.

CHAPTER ELEVEN

That night, Ishtar met with the animals and plants which were assigned to assist her during the conquest. They needed to devise a plan quickly. She knew the culprit causing the destruction of the continent and the reasons thereof. She also knew that she couldn't work without their assistance as it was evident that Memnon had destructive weapons both for the carnal and spiritual warfare. Their plan was to be simple; move many citizens from the mainland to the newly discovered Area 51. Some believed that this was a new space where aliens lived. However, during her escape from the human traffickers, this was the land into which Ishtar fell through the portal and found Oracle Marble and the beautiful animal and human dynasty. A place of Holy Communion amongst all beings from the galaxies beyond. Area 51 was where the trail was to be found. The place which evaded Memnon for so many decades. There, lay the answers of the world. There, him and every other being would find the gold they seek. Before executing their plan, there was a need to reassure the citizens about their health concerns. Strange viruses were released and the testing grounds for medicine identified as Alkebulan. There were equally conflicting conspiracy theories making rounds to pressure the living to conform to one of the other. Ishtar had a responsibility towards the people to ascertain them that help was available and that their cry was not in vain. For this task they needed Grootslang, the serpent from South Africa to initiate contact with the entire continent. She didn't need to tell him what to do. That night, after the consultative meeting, Grootslang took to action with his offsprings followed by many reptiles they set up camp outside one of the highest mountains on the continent. As Ishtar adorned them with powers, there was no delay in traveling from one end of the continent to the other. Grootslang and his offspring made their way underground to Mount Kilimanjaro. In the quiet hour of the night, the offspring started to bang on the ground with their tails. Because of their size, the tales created pulsations which were heard all over the continent. People were frightened. Those closest to the site thought it was an earthquake, others thought that it was thunderstorms. As the pulses increased, an opening appeared at the top of the mountain. From beneath, a tall golden stave exited and stood tall on the mountain peak. While Kilimanjaro was the tallest on the continent, the golden stave added more inches of height into the sky. The curious few that came out of their houses could see the golden staff shining on top of the mountain. Grootslang slowly mounted the staff and wrapped himself in the well-known spiral which confirms human DNA structures, around it. Thus, creating an illusion of the ancient sign of healing, back on the Alkebulan soil. There was confusion amongst the people. The sign could be seen all over Alkebulan as it was magnified with powers unknown to the world. Whoever gazed his eye to the mountains could see its reflection. To the old and wise, the message was clear and they celebrated. To the young and unwise, the message was unclear and thus declared sinister. In many manipulated minds, it was a sign from the evil one. The distorted script writer, knowing of the days of tomorrow, had made provision for the revelations from the world beyond. As he could see beyond the seas and the spaces, he captured those memories in his books such that people were misinformed. They believed so much in his words that they identified the symbol with evil. While Grootslang stood in services to pronounce the dawn of healing, the people he was to serve called him evil and turn their heads away in fear. People came from all other parts of the world to witness the sign. Scientists and modern magicians were called in to examine and explain the origins of the symbol. However, they could not get to close because Grootslang was alive and not a statue. As it was written, time was needed to judge the truth. Though people wanted to comprehend the reality, science was not ready to see the truth reflected. Their consciousness was to be ignited and reconciled with the true knowledge of life. Furthermore, to find answers regarding Grootslang, science was investigating past experience to find solutions to present day occurrences, while the enlightened few simply followed the divine compass of time. Thus, only those with the true gift and wisdom could identify its true purpose and align with it accordingly. The light workers were at work, swiftly they would move amongst the people, from city to city and remove those that saw the healer for what he was and received their healing. It was not time to broadcast out loud to everyone. Those that sought for the truth were bound to receive and those that remained idle, equally served in ignorance.

Memnon was beneath the ground, working and experimenting with his tools so he missed the early opportunities to see the developments on the continent. While he was busy looking for ways to capture Ishtar, she was actively changing things outside. When he finally learned that there was a statue erected on Mount Kilimanjaro, the movement of Ishtar was deeply advanced in changing the tides. Their next move was the World conference. The conference was aimed at discussing new lending regulations for Alkebulan and put sanctions on those countries which didn't comply with the new decisions of the world governing bodies. The conferences were broadcast over all news outlets during a time that people from other continents were starting to see reason. Thus, governments were receiving pressure from their citizens under the leadership from civil societies concern with human rights and independent activists. As the human eye was turning tide, it saw injustice for what it was. No longer where people concerned with skin colour or destruction of humanity. There was an increase in mixed race marriages. Children born of Alkebulanian and Moneylenders blood were growing up and taking center stage. They were superseding the power of Memnon by being truthful and loving the world genuinely. They were raising and institutionalizing political reform. These children stood up in support of the motherland. Under such pressures, the greedy leaders were trying to meet to disguise yet another plan of world rule. When the eye is blinded by greed, it can't see brightly even when light is offered. Consequently, knowing that they were in too deep the leaders pushed on to make new policies. Just like in the past, when the great Emperors of Alkebulan were called by the Oracle at the sound of a new horn. The leaders traveled with their assistants outside of the continents and respective countries. The meeting place, Namibia. Over the past decades, meetings of such proportion used to take place in the western world but after the devastation caused during the last peace conferences hijacked by protestors, the mighty powers agreed it was best to have the meetings on the Alkebulan soil. This was done in order to divert the attention away from their front door into the heart of Alkebulan. In their eyes, Alkebulan was the dumping ground for anything. Its people were used as guinea pigs for each and every scientific research. Its soil; their source of income and progression. Its space their property to destroy or use as amusement. Therefor when the world powers threatened each other and logged heads in a cold war to determine who is mightier than the other, it was again safe to move such meetings away from their respective countries to protect their citizens. The ever greedy sons of the Alkebulan soil simply held their hands out for a few golden plates which were stolen from their soil in return for silence, so that the conference could take place in its space. Namibia was viewed in many aspects as the epitome of change and opportunity. Not that there were no greater and more powerful states to contend with but, for the same reason, the gods have chosen to send Ishtar to reincarnate in that space. It was a young independent country with its leaders still learning the robes of politics. The population was small and the vast landscapes not inhibited by many people. Hence, any experiment, war plant or whatever the world powers saw fit, could easily be erected and executed within that space. However, the leaders had been logging heads for a long time. They were under currents of mistrust. As they were all aiming for world dominion, no superpower was willing to relinquish the power on Alkebulan. The inner strive was slowly becoming visible to the citizens as their joint conspiracies were discovered and plans were failing. Leaders raised against each other shifting blame from one source to the other and in the wake of such times, it was evident that each had an ulterior motive in changing venues of meetings. Either they hoped to assassin each other and blame it on Alkebulan, or they wanted to outsmart each other by scheming with the Alkebulanian leaders. Hence they all prepared for a possible outbreak of war as they journeyed to Alkebulan. The idea of the meeting venue was not just suitable for the world leaders, it suited Memnon with his base in Namibia as he was certain it will draw Ishtar to his doorstep.

Ishtar was certain that her plan needed to be executed by influencing her people. Due to distance, the Alkebulan leaders arrived earlier than the others. Off course the protocol teams had to put measures in place to safeguard their presidents while the Alkebulan brothers were just moving from one door to the next to visit each other. Hence, they were two days early, which was good enough for Ishtar to engage their attention. That night, she implored the services of Tikoloshe, the ancient gremlin used by shamans as messengers. They had powers to torture or manipulate humans such that they could act in the way prescribed. The Tikoloshes could see very well in darkness and once given the particulars of a target, they were able to track them down no matter the distance and boundaries. Ishtar thus spoke to the source and it multiplied itself into 54 tiny images which had to hunt down each president of Alkebulan. While they were all caught up in their hotel rooms across the city of Windhoek, the Namibian capital city, the little creatures entered each room exactly at the same time. Making use of its powers, the security guards who thought they heard screams inside could not enter the rooms as a dark power was holding it close. They heard fierce voices and arguments but couldn't decipher it because the language of the Tikoloshe is only transmitted in an interpretable sense for its chosen receiver. Some groomed through guerilla warfare and others empowered by great shamans and sangomas from the soil were not an easy match. They fought against the beast with all might, perhaps they would have worn that night but their own spirits have been weakened over the years by the choice of lifestyles they led. Alkebulan leaders with all their spiritual gifts showered by the creator where heavily manipulated by the world systems initiated by Memnon such that they could not fought back against the Tikoloshe. It was a sad night for the ancestors to see how weak their sons have indeed become to witness a defeat from a gremlin that listens to the voice of the powerful master only, a gremlin who is in fact scared of humans as they were made slaves by them for millions of years. Yet, today they too could overpower the son who is supposed to hold the power of truth to subdue any evil formed against it. They bowed in defeat to the demands of the Tikoloshe as they could not stand the physical torture. The next morning they woke up as if in a dream all bearing scratch marks and various tiny signs under their heavy cloths as if they were fighting with millions of little kids. They were all ashamed to know and admit that they were not only defeated by the world system but also caught off guard by the supernatural forces as they allowed their minds to be polluted. In the meeting room to discuss strategies to host the other presidents, instead a new war was created. Instead of agreeing to strategies for its people, the 54 presidents of Alkebulan were divided. There was no trust as they have all recognized the Tikoloshe, they were sons of the soil after all who grew up in societies were the gremlin was portrayed as an evil devise to rob others of their hard earned success or as family protectors against charms from the evil eye. By identifying the gremlin, they couldn't trust each other. Each of the leaders thought that one or the other brought his charms to confuse the masses and gain favour in the eyes of the foreigner, to gain more power in Alkebulan. Forgetting the message of unity the Tikoloshe was trying to bring to their attention, they cried foul and spit in each other's faces and before the mighty jets from the west and east could land, they packed their bags and returned to their respective countries. The President of Namibia was confused as, his country was burning under one catastrophic attack to another. People were being killed by forces he could not identify, some under the disguise of governors who have died some years ago and others, through unexplained means. He hoped to be the head driving unity between the Alkebulan leaders but stood with his hands on the head as the new events unfolded. He equally felt the wrath of the gremlin the night before and had his doubts about his brothers, but he still needed to host the other visitors who were already traveling thus could not be contacted to turn their planes around. Now sitting without a cabinet of Alkebulan leaders, he had to make a decision.

In the world beneath; the one they all referred to as Kumta (Area 51), Ishtar sits by the feet of Oracle Marble. With a sigh she questions, "How am I to go about all this?" The oracle chuckles softly and pats the young woman on her head. "With time, answers will reveal themselves, but you are aware that it needs the human in you to find solutions and not the godly figure don't know?" The young woman looked at the oracle with evident frustrations. We knew the culprits, we knew the reasons, and we also knew the outcome. So, why can't they just deal with it swiftly she wonders, why go through all this turmoil? Why loosing lives of people and prolonging the end? At her thoughts, the oracle laughed out loud. "Well child, but you know better. You can't end something which has been created never to end. This is their world. Amma's covenant with them was that they make it their own and govern it sensibly. The quest here is simply for them to understand the term sensibly. They can't end their existence nor can we, unless you end the cycle of reincarnation which is infact the essence of who we all are. Just like all the other species belong in the galaxies beyond, so do these little uncivilized few. Do you remember the days of Planet XL-3? Oh what a sight it was to witness! They stumbled more than Planet C-53, there was a time that only ten were alive and breaking all rules of new days mating. They repopulated their world. Today, with machinery and all they have, they created a new dynasty where hope never cease. Each and everyday they grow closer to enlightenment and godliness". The two laugh as they recall the birth times of the other planets and this convinced Ishtar again that there was hope for Planet C-53, and not just Alkebulan but the entire planet. It could be done with proper structures to rebuild out of Alkebulan. "Yes, this is what Amma wants, thus so be it." She mumbled.

That night after seeking audiences with the Oracle, Ishtar experienced yet again a pull that plunged her into another town. She found herself amongst many living in an unfinished industrial park. Though some of the housing units were decently covered, it proofed a less conducive environment in many ways, yet the people made to do with the little as factories were run down and rusty and only two were fully functional. In fact, these were the energy sources of the community as they produced steel to the entire country. Even though a good stream of income was made from the sales, it could not provide adequately for the development of the town. There was always something broken to fix. Consequently, the town council could not progress beyond fixing to developing new infrastructures or so they were informed at each town council meeting. There were a few lucky people in the town with decent accommodation and Ishtar struck a luck and found herself amongst them. After being thrown out of her foster home, she found her way to the nearest church for prayers and guidance. There she was met by a missionary couple that took her under their wings. The wife was certain that Ishtar was god sent and held a divine purpose. Under the authority of this couple, Ishtar was introduced to a new way of thinking and worshiped to an unseen God. At first, she could not place her inner feelings and the effect the teachings had on her. There were times that it brought peace; mostly when they talked about the greatest love. At other times she was confused and conflicted about the harsh punishments and wars people were subjected to. One thing was certain, whichever way she tried to interpret the history of the faithful people, she was certain that their united lack of understanding the principles and history thereof led to the confusion they faced now in the world. She would sit for hours upon hours reflecting upon the various religious practices found on earth and mostly here on the continent of Alkebulan. She found that they could at least agree about two things, no matter how misplaced they were, they all believed that there was a God, a higher power and an afterlife. How each chose to get there was the sole reason earthlings were at war with each other. If that portion was to be removed, Ishtar bet they would have co-existed in love.

Soon, the day that the Town's mayor called for a community meeting came. To the surprise of the local people he rocked up to the meeting with a fleet of flashy cars. There were bodyguards surrounding him as he passed through the crowd into the roofless town hall. Everyone, except the locals, was wearing sunglasses. With the morning rains having subsided, it was a bright cloudy day. Thus, with no visible sun, it was a wonder why they were wearing shades. "Gmpf! Today they fear looking in our eyes," someone mumbled near Ishtar. "No my dear, they are hiding their own shame," another responded. So the observations went off from one to the other. Ishtar lend out her ear very well to understand the depth of the people's resentment towards their own leaders. This was surely no form of dictatorship. She heard that the government and local authority leaders were ruthless clan of scammers. They have passed the extremes of corruption, money laundry and sold out their birthright to foreign nations. All that was left, if not sold already, were their souls to the devil. They were worse than the vultures of the soil, demolishing even the dry bones. Under such leadership the country crumbled. The little life that has remained in parts of the country; that is what they now seek out in the name of reformation. Ishtar looked around and all she could see was crumbling and deteriorating buildings with no windows or doors and partially roofed houses and no trees, potholes decorated the streets. They were so extreme that even the Mercedes drivers of the Mayor had to play "hide and seek" to steer the car on decent patches. Yet the people turned up for the meeting. Just three months ago heavy rains destroyed their water pipes and the town was smelling under the lack of water. They very mayor who called for the meeting relocated with his family to the capital city for the interim, until the water crisis sorts itself out miraculously. People were contracting strange deceases and under the extreme conditions good healthcare was a far sighted dream. But no there were the ever willing, ever voting, patriotic citizens. Having laid a red carpet for their masters, a high table laid with beautiful bouquet of flowers (imported) as there were no flower shop around town. Water bottles and mint sweets on place holders for the nighty, while the needy had no chairs to sit on. Let alone decent shade to cover their weary bodies. Ishtar looked around and sighed. "Would she ever understand this species? What is she to make of all this ridiculousness?" She has never come across a species with so much untapped brain power and energy that filled earth with the best vegetation abilities. Yet, they remained the one clueless beings in the entire universe. For the first time, she stands in awe while wondering if she should applaud them for stupidity or admire their ignorance. Surely, this is one of the species dying because of lack of knowledge, all by their own design. How then, do they hope to be rescued by the god's they pray too?" she wondered. As she was moving out of thought, something propelled her to look behind. There was a young woman standing with arms crossed to the chest, looking at her smiling. Their eyes met briefly, but in that instant, recognition of spirit was made. Her lips moved but no sound came. Ishtar turned towards the front just to ascertain her eye sight and looked back slowly again. The woman has moved an inch closer in that instant and whispered to Ishtar.

"Run and hide"

At hearing that, Ishtar quickly looked around and could see no danger. She quickly turned back to question the lady but the other was gone. She slowly moved to the back of the crowd searching for the lady. Just as she got closer to the last group of people, someone screamed.

"Jesus, Jesus! What is this?" he screamed. Right behind them appeared a large war craft hanging in the air. It was too close to the ground hence forcing strong winds blowing towards the people. People started running for cover. Ishtar also ran around the nearest wall. Surprised, scared and out of breath she sat there wondering what was happening. Why were there low flying aircrafts in their town, much less at the meeting point? She wondered.

Run the strange lady said to her. Why did she even select her? She wondered, but there was no time. She had to find a way out of this place. Possibly a way out of the town as well. As panic raised around her the vibration of fear lit her up literally and she started glowing like the sun. One of the men running with the crowd saw her and stopped in his track, looked at her surprised and rushed to her side. He thought that the war craft might have hit her with some kind of toxic substance and set her body on fire. Luckily, others around them didn't notice in their rush and it only appeared for a brief moment. He came up to Ishtar and tried to stretch out his hands to help her but in that second, she disappeared and all that remained was a dark hole through the wall. With a shocking surprise, the man looked around him, shook his head a couple of times in wonder and started running again when he remembered what was happening around them. Unfortunately, they were not alone. Another dressed in black was also watching and he slowly replaced his sunglasses on his face and turned towards one of the fleet of cars. Inside, he took out his phone and dialed a number. The receiver on the other side didn't wait on a voice message. He spoke first. "Thank you James. Now it's time to prepare the others."

When Memnon realized that Ishtar was gaining ground to rediscover the powers hidden on Alkebulanian soil, he instructed his son's all over the world to take action. His knights were few but powerful because they held the money which was controlling the world. They were the ones sponsoring presidents into office. Referendums were changed in their favour each time a new president was to be elected. They had their hands into all political parties, be it left or right wing, their puppets were paid to serve according to their instructions. The biggest scientific and research organisations in the world were funded by these handful giants. The world banks and mineral producing companies all belonged to them. As Memnon's offspring were getting out of hand and trying to play the safe world cards instead of following his blue print, he called his final trump and summoned the Mighty 12. From the Americas, Europe and Asia they came together by night in the heart of Namibia. Though there was turbulence felt all over Alkebulan, it was still barely safe to meet in that space. Many reasons worked in their favour because the people living in that space were very reluctant. Though they would observe injustice, they never joined forces to raise against their government. Their immediate neighbours and rest of Alkebulan were known to have fierce uprisings against injustice which would have them tore down any administrative or governing structures if they were not heard. They would have bloody wars and fight against any system with everything they had in their power. The few populace of Namibia was deeply divided on ethnic grounds to be able to come together as a people to fight for their country. Hence, others misused their gullibility to orchestrate their own agendas while hosted on the soil. It was a sad case to witness, for the citizens were but a mere handful, living on one of the richest pieces of dirt on the Alkebulanian soil. They had everything working in their favour and their colonizers made sure to create excellent infrastructures they could rely upon. The governing systems were intact and the general livelihood was better prepared when they took over to lead themselves. They proofed to be no different than their siblings of neighbouring countries lending out their ear to the money lenders and sitting in the counsel of the unwise. However, they all had genuine concerns about the continent because the atrocities taking place all over were harming their source of income. For good five years after the fall out at the supposed world conference they started meeting silently while rebuilding the Organisation of Alkebulan Union and sharing best practices of governance to restore their countries. It was not an easy tasks because during the last summit and rebellion, many suffered severely as their main cities were bombed and countless lives were lost. To this day, they are still working to recover from the attacks from unknown forces as no country claimed responsibility thereof. The Mighty 12 who were Memnon's direct beneficiaries from developed countries were all witnessing the changes which were taking place on the continent. They were involved in funding some exercises but increasingly, the governing entities were changing. Young and vibrant leaders were taking over positions on the continent and people were starting to distance themselves from the mighty influences and rediscovering their own identity. Through various platforms and with the aid of Pan Alkebulan Organisations, people were re-educated about the history of Alkebulan and its people making use of various sources those with the know-how dig into the past and exposed history which was omitted from mainstream education. Colonialism ascertained that citizens of Alkebulan were taught how to glorify the successes of their colonizers thus its own history was either hide or not recorded. However, with the rise of change, literary works emerged during post colonialism and spread over the world. Through intensive research, they found the truth which was hidden from them for many years. With that truth, the colonizers were exposed just as much as they twisted the history and creation of the world. The colonizer's mastermind to pronounce every discovery made by Alkebulanians as their own. The new generations were educated to know who the real discoverers of machinery, internets, architecture, medicine and even religion was. Children were reconditioned at homes and away from centers which were manipulating their minds and increasingly, black consciousness was rising to the forefront, but, it was at a cost. While the East was silently working on measures to take over Alkebulan in a friendly disguise, they fashioned new capitalist practices to invest heavily in the Alkebulanian development. As developmental assistance was stopped by the West in an effort to curb Alkebulan's disobedience to follow orders, the siblings were rising up to the understanding that they were treated as puppets on their own soil. The woman's place was being restored and she was included in decision making positions of the governments all over the continent. Genuine concerns about the future of the continent was discussed because the mothering figures were involved and they were repenting from their error of selfish acts and standing together to raise a new continent, the Alkebulanian way; where children were raised by everyone, as they belonged to everyone and for the good of the continent.

While they were in the process to rediscover their worth and implement new structures for intercontinental relations, the Mighty 12 meeting on the soil of Namibia were worried. Alkebulanians were multiplying beyond measure, so did the other nations. The increasing populace on the face of the earth was threatening their strongholds as each new kid on the block refused to adhere to their manifestos, not only on the Alkebulanian soil were people moving away from the memorization the western powers hold. They wanted to be free from them on all grounds, be it economical, mental or simply distance themselves from the dreams which didn't favour their citizens, each wanting to make their space great again. The Mighty 12 were responsible for many atrocities which were taking place in the world. From the inception of world wars, pandemics and so called natural disasters which were all manmade while carried out by them to reduce the increasing number of people. A smaller population in all parts of the world was manageable but with the increasing numbers, they risk losing everything they have built for the new world order. Furthermore, there was also the disagreements internally as each one had their own plans of ruling the world.

They all harbored in their minds the same thought to one day outsmart Memnon and take over leadership. What kept them at bay was that none of the initiated few went up in rank to be trusted with the ultimate secrets that Memnon had. Each one thus made a mental note to seek out the truth before executing Memnon to take the lead. Hence, they worked together with differing minds. At this meeting it was thus decided to release another virus that would have a much higher impact than the others before. As foretold years back by an American president, they released an airborne virus, one that spread over a short span of time to kill millions of people all around the world. This was a virus created from substances of animals, blocking the respiratory systems of humans and taking lives at alarming speed. With the release of the virus, they utilized the internet and social media to propagate the virus such that people doubt its effect. This caused fear in some people. They owned all leading organizations responsible for humanitarian aid and health, thus, they could easily manipulate the information released. People were misinformed about the usage of effective drugs as new discoveries to treat the virus were nabbed in the butt so that it couldn't reach the world on time. The economies of the world suffered as the world came to a standstill as they were locked down, productions couldn't take place, and businesses couldn't operate. People couldn't live their lives the way they wanted to because fear was the best messenger and the responsible persons made sure that they released propaganda every other hour. The world stopped talking about anything other than the virus and how to find a cure for it. These trying times were in favour of Alkebulan. For yet again, though the producers of the virus knew how to treat and stop it. They didn't have sufficient proof that their inventions were to work. In the background, Alkebulanian all over the world with expertise in the medical field were breaking records in finding antidotes. In the western worlds, they were still not named as the Caucasians took the glory. But with the help of the active Pan Alkebulanian friends, word was spread that motivated the leaders of the continent and the underlining messages were decoded. Experts of the soil started asking relevant questions. Why was every new drug tested on Alkebulanians? What was it within their physic that overpowered the efforts of destruction posed by the greedy? Alkebulan went back in time and studied its gifts. They produced their own remedies against the dreaded disease. While one country discovered the herbal cure, others didn't lay back in silence. As the two biggest entities were fighting over the ownership of the virus and demand payment leaders of the soil reopened their eyes to the truth. Their offspring were maltreated in both the countries on the forefront of the virus war. Their resources were owned by these countries and their livelihood depended from these countries. It was a difficult time for them to make decisions to save their people. The west pushed for vaccinations to be tested in Alkebulan and by refusing, the already crumbling economies would be dealt with dismissals of funding. By refusal, they would lose alliances which were needed to keep them flooding above the waters. They couldn't reject the west as their funding depended on them, likewise, they couldn't reject the east as their major infrastructures were in their hands. However, there were the brave brothers that stepped out to say no to both countries. For them, it was about the human factor and not the money. It was a ride or die situation for them to rescue their dignity as people. Alkebulanians in diaspora had immeasurable struggles, they were hated because of their skin colour and treated less than the animals they consumed. Hence, the leaders with wisdom started to stand up for their people. Though many were heartbroken that it had to take crumbling economies and a virus to rescue their people, it was not late for the leaders to write petitions to repatriate their people at any costs from the diaspora. They started caring for their people and created relive funds to support them, not only during the pandemic but also started dialogues for future development of the continent. They started to advocate for withdrawals from many organisations including the World Health Organisation and invested in their herbal plants. They refused medical supplies from other countries and relied upon their own health care services. Not all were on board though and this created strive amongst the peers. The host country, offering meeting spaces also accepted the medical gifts from the east during that time that nature took its cause and healed itself silently from the harsh conditions imposed on it by the humans. The oceans were clearing, dust disappeared from the sky, the air which the people needed to breath to curb any disease was cleared outside while they were all lock down inside. Animals enjoyed the peace and tranquility and sang praises to the gods. For once, the world came to an abrupt standstill and at that time many people reflected on life but also made others more stubborn than before while the truth was staring them right in the their faces. Presidents became childish and the communities around mocked them for not using common sense. The true identities of the human race came to fore during this time and Ishtar could really dig deep within them to finally understand how divided they were. It was not going to be an easy task to reunite the thoughts of the people as they were deeply divided and manipulated by systems created over hundreds of years. Their recovery to ultimate freedom and transformation was not going to happen over time. It would require another thousand years to reshape them. She didn't know if they would have so much time but the evidence of eternal life was in the proof of nature. Each and everytime its inhabitants produced destruction, it found a way to reinvent itself. The latest pandemic was a lesson to learn from. Humans bounded by fear and misunderstanding of life, lock themselves away from the world. Mother Nature smiled at the senselessness of her children and took time out to nurture the soil back to its original strength. Those that could see, realized that nature was a universal entity on its own and not theirs to destroy. The human heart was able to murder and remove each other from the face of the earth, but nature in itself was powerful. Given the space and time of a mere two to four months it restored itself back to its glory without the interference of humans. What does that say about humanity? How deep routed is their conviction of longevity or do they subscribe to transience? Who needs who to co-exist on the piece of dirt, which is never granted the respect it deserves?

The virus was finally content and people returned to a new normal. The Mighty 12 lost the battle of cashing in on a vaccine and they were not happy as some Alkebulanian countries succumbed under the pressure others stood their grounds. These were the countries with higher population rates and with intellectual capacity banked across the world. They knew that the pressures of the Mighty 12 wasn't going to bring them to their knees because they were relying on human interest which they secured during the pandemic. This made the Mighty 12 realize that the time has approached for reckoning. Alkebulan or parts of it has matured with mighty resistance. They were probing questions and repossessing their identity. With their economies scattered, government buildings, airports, harbours, agricultural fields, mines and the entire civil services impounded by the money lenders. They were homeless within their own land as the decisions of the leaders who chose not to listen to the soft whisper of their children caused them dearly. They robbed the hungry and plunged them deeper into poverty. Hearts were not happy and were rising up against defeated leaders, as the Mighty 12 were pulling in all directions and not listening to the commands of Memnon he made use of this time to single Ishtar out to war. He was aware of the thoughts that each and every one of the Mighty 12 were harbouring. Working with any one of them would mean revealing his ultimate secret and face total destruction. Thus, when they couldn't reach consensus and each member worked out from the conference on its own, he knew that the time came for him to fight his course alone. For many decades he was worked tirelessly to groom men into power so that they could stand with him. But over and over they failed him, as they all had the same heart which couldn't be governed by another. He made a vow during the conference of the emperors of Alkebulan millions of years ago to rule the world and all that was within it, even if it meant to be the last man standing. After millions of efforts, great successes and all, he was not ready to face a defeat. He knew the only source standing between him and the ultimate glory was Ishtar. To hell with the politicians, money lenders and greedy fools he thought. He has made them all and even if they tried to outweigh him they were not able. For he had the power to return, again and again to the world until his mission was achieved. Their purpose has been served and they were not needed any more. Through social media, Memnon started uploading videos of Ishtar. He manipulated the images that demonized her being and post it all. Fashionable with every new conspiracy or religious attack, social media got hold of the information and spread it like wild fire. Curiosity was ignited and also the source of all the worlds' troubles was found in Ishtar. Memnon released his scripts again, with information of the coming of a new vicious ruler, hinting towards Ishtar. Those in Namibia who recognized her quickly spread word of their association with her. It was either about the good deeds or the mistakes that she made which were now ripped it out of context. The past few month's positive developments falling through the cracks immediately.

Alkebulan had a painful history about tribal and ethnicity fueled wars where people of independent countries turned upon its own. In the heat of the moment, foreign interferences were forgotten and people turned to disagree on every developmental and political front. Those white lighter skins were ridiculed in some parts of the continent and even killed under a pretense of cleansing the country from bad influences. Though light skinned people existed before the foreign invasion, they were targeted as a reminder of what the foreigners did prior to independence. People thought that they were the favoured races and thus treated fairly by the foreigners, not deserving to part take in the new freedom pleasures, while forgotten that this people may also have experience the pains of colonialism. In other parts of the continent, this very light skinned people thought themselves as the first class citizens and treated the darker with contempt. All this fueled resistance amongst each other and started a civil war at times ending with devastating genocides. As history had it, the Alkebulanians divided in tribes also had a history of tribal wars where one tribe thought itself more superior than the other. Where people were classified on baseless prejudice and excluded from progressive support systems during new governments led by various political parties. These would be political parties with strong ties leaning towards a specific tribe. It was a well-known fact that people on the continent only united during wars against the foreigner. However, when matters were closer to home and the cause their own, they would jump back into tribal favoritism and judgement. Namibia thus suffered with undercurrents of tribal differences when Ishtar was portrayed as the evil doer. First to surface its ugly head was tribalism and people started looking at her features which would be the determining factor of her fate. The ruling political party was said to have a majority support from a tribe mainly based in the north but its current leader was from a clan closely linked to that of Ishtar. Thus, already a divide in leadership existed. Some people blamed the president to be the cause of all the economic and corrupt activities that brought the country to its knees way before his time because he hailed from a less favoured clan. Other political entities were promoting a corrupt system which was pushing all government developmental activities in favour of its own. This divide was felt in all circles of movement in the country as the false pride and patriotism leading the country into more depression. Hence, it was not a surprise when people asked from where Ishtar hailed as the first thing during her demonization by Memnon. Some people surged their shoulders and said nothing good was to be expected from that tribe. Others stood tall in celebrating her being in favour of their achievements as a clan. The undercurrents growing overtime spewed like a volcano all around the country and the elders fought in the parliament and, in the communities and villages. Some were killed in the process and, exiled. But the biggest riot that started was the one where they destroyed their own property and infrastructures while fighting against each other; a foolish act Ishtar could never understand as those rising up to protest about something always did in their own backyards and destroyed their own. True to the Alkebulanian proverb that says, when elephants fights the grass suffers. Young in independence the country had war veterans with fresh memories of war with men and women from both sides of the frontline and the troops that fought for the country and others that defend it from the rebels. During that war, many were tortured based on propaganda of spying against their own. The exiled warrior thought nothing of the one fighting under pressure by the colonial system. During war, people stood together under the same burner but with different motives and this was not different in Namibia. After independence, instead of seeking reconciliation and starting a debate of forgiveness and healing, people simply plunged into a new unfamiliar world and proceeded without addressing the pains experienced during the war. According allowing the wounds to simmer under the shallow skin. Memnon thus created an opportunity to spark yet another fire amongst the people who didn't trust each other. A people who thought that one was more deserving than the other to exist in the country. He simply sat back and watched them destroy each other. For years, there were talks of building a new resistance amongst the different tribes. Led by painful experiences and unforgotten hate which was first instituted by the foreigner, the people now promoted the idea of taking up arms. They were all stubborn as they could all lean on the expertise of either freedom fighters or defenders of the foreign systems. Insults were hurled from all sides and under increase pressure, the country stood at the verge of a civil war. Memnon smiled as he looked down on the foolishness of mankind. Their stubborn nature and intelligence now causing a greater divide than he had anticipated. They were going to make it easy for him to execute his plan. Looking at their actions now, he realized that the biggest and mightiest weapon of mass destruction for Alkebulanians was not diseases or military weapons. It was their tribal convictions. All that was needed was to keep fueling the fire by promoting tribal propaganda and they would rise against each other, so fiercely that they would kill each other. They had the military weapons to execute the kill. Gang members were buying it on the black market sold by corrupt employers of the defense structures. Illegal arm dealings were also taking place all around the world as each country stupidly thought to invest more in security rather than other developmental initiatives. Thus with enough ammunition, each man felt empowered and stronger than the other and unfortunately, neither Ishtar or the ones that has orchestrated the war was the target.

Ishtar carried all that was human in the body temple, thus, she fiercely experienced carnal behavior. Her feelings were hurt and she was contemplating to halt the divine mission. These were not deserving people to be rescued, she reasoned. They ridiculed and tainted her image and as a goddess, this was the biggest insult to her being and she was not ready to be ridiculed by a species lesser than herself. No different from the mankind, she was equally allowing her carnal feelings to take over her reasoning and sound judgement. In a moment of rage she stepped away from the people and the mission. For two full years, the people fought each other as a full fledge civil uprising broke out. The government was weakened and unable to make an executive decision as no one gave ear to the other. People were angry for many things as it was no longer about Ishtar, now people were just rising up and loitering because of one or the other injustice they had experience over the 30 years of independence. A sad time thus laid ahead for the people. During days of sanity, they saw how the economy collapsed further. The once strong currency dropped and ranked as garbage and the education and health systems destroyed. Jobs were lost and massive depression swept all over the country. Its neighbours looked on the presidents and remembered the humiliation caused by the gremlin at their last meeting. As many blamed the Namibian president for it, no help was afforded to him during his time of need. They simply turned their heads away and foolishly decided that the country should sort out its personal matters on its own. International relations were broken as every country was going through pressures of its own. The only happy person out of this was Memnon.

Ishtar sat in a jungle in a faraway tropical forest, out of sight of people. Amongst her were the animals designated to war alongside her. They were not human and knew how to keep their oaths. They swore to assist Ishtar to execute the rescue plan and they were willing to stick with it even if it meant to wait on her to clear her mind and return to normal. The only one not present was the Groot Slang that remained in his position on the mountain. Now forgotten by everyone as they were busy messing up the country, only a few found time during the civil uprisings to turn their faces to seek the truth in his direction. For those few, he remained in the position. For Ishtar and the animal's time was not of essence. Two years simply could mean two minutes, hours or seconds in Ishtar's original world and she forgot to stay on track with the human clock. Upon inquiry from the Oracle, she woke up from her slumber, only to realize that so much time has passed. Under the guidance of the Medicanice priestesses that traced her location she was reintroduced to the power of forgiveness and made to understand that the only source of bridging all wars was the heart of man that truly understood what it meant to forgive another for his errors and embrace them in healing. This was the one thing Ishtar had in common with the citizens of Alkebulan. They were a difficult people to forget the past and find true healing. This was not entirely out of their own doing. The systems were designed in such a way that they celebrated every bad experience as a memorial or commemoration day. A day at which they would meet in huge crowds to remember the by gone era of pain; a device of Memnon to keep their heads in the darkness. Ishtar listened to the advice from those that walked long in the body temple of man and took time to reflect on her own weaknesses. In the wake of time she looked within and identified her flaws which kept her from finally transitioning into the being she was supposed to be to master the rescue plan. During the past thirty years, she kept who she was separated. The body was not aligned with the spirit. Each did what they fought to be the best on the given time. There was no coherence in her presence and the two forces carnal and spirit were always fighting against each other. She realized that this was what each and every human being must have been experiencing. The knowledge of self as a whole entity and not separated as body and spirit, was the main reason they could not evolve beyond the limitations they saw on earth. She now understood that the only true way of rescuing these people was by giving them all an opportunity to strife towards discovering of themselves. With this realization, Ishtar's transformation was complete. The next day she woke up in a perfect being as the true daughter of both worlds. Worlds united within her as the source, opening her eyes to the wonders of Amma. She stood in awe as she could finally understand why Amma had made such a deep binding covenant with the human race on earth. For they were indeed exalted above all other species, because they were the only ones belonging to this world. They were the ultimate masters of their destiny, not the ancestors, not the gods. Ishtar stood there in the full regalia of Oyá the Orisha of winds, lighting and violent storms, death and rebirth she stood high above the people. In ancient Alkebulan, Orisha was a spirit sent by higher divinities for the guidance of all creation and of humanity in particular on how to live and be successful on Earth. With all that presence included within her own powers as the goddess Ishtar she stood infront of them all. On her head, she carried a crown made from a cow's horn and the feathers of a Turaco; symbolizing the presence of the cow horn. The cow in itself was a symbol of wealth, fertility and authority the significance of it was to be able to withstand colonization and westernization in Alkebulan. It also signified masculinity and as the women were raising up to free their sons, it was the perfect symbol to carry. In Alkebulan royal courts, the horn was presented as a token of respect to chiefs by warriors who may have travelled far to fight in wars. It was a voice imitation to relay messages which could not be spoken. Ishtra thus needed to carry the symbol in silence to represent the purpose of her actions. The feathers presented a public distinction of courage and high esteem. This crown off course was carried on the head of the goddess with recognizable kinky hair; a common trait for people with Alkebulanian decent. The hair texture may have evolved in an adaptive need to protect the people against the strong UV radiation. Ishtar also carried a butterfly on her right shoulder which symbolized the transformation that the people were about to receive. The unattached golden circle above her head signified the angelic presence of spiritual forces to help them along the new journey. Now fully equip to lead the people, she presented herself available for the war at hand.

CHAPTER TWELVE

Ishtar looked at the allies from the animal kingdom and said. "The people of the land say that those that walk under the ground will never see the fairyland. It is time for us to be seen and heard in the land so that the people can make a final decision. Destiny is in their hands and the land belongs to them. Whichever way they choose will be entirely by their own doing. Time is equally against us as we need to return to our own space." They agreed with her and the war strategy was once more revisited before the first animals took to flight. That night, strange noises were heard on the soil of the continent. Adze the vampire and Kongamato took the first journey to gather all the birds to form an air force. Through the leaves of the Whistling Thorn, word was send all around for the wise to prepare. It was always known in Alkebulan that every whisper was soaked up and spread by the whistling thorn such that the wise always warn people not to share secrets in the open. However, over time, all this information has been forgotten. The wise eyes kept looking to the trees and inquired from them for direction. Hence it was no different on that fateful day to receive news from the trees but, in the midst of the wise eyes, there were those that have conformed to the changing times and changed their alliances from good to bad. The ones that chose to work with the evil masters and sell out on the wisdom of men. They stood in the counsel of the presidents but also with the common men who betrayed his brother for monetary gain. Thus, understanding that the eminent war was to be fought both on land and in the spiritual realm, each man went out to consult his own. Throughout the continent, ancient shrines were uncovered. The wise ones started calling out to the gods of their land. Incantations and many rituals were observed on the land but, the gods remained silent and were no longer willing to speak to the children of the soil. The decision to send Ishtar into their world was the final step towards either their reformation or destruction. The ancestors were also silent as they could no longer turn back to guide their children. Dark clouds rose and covered the continent. Ear deafening thunder was heard on the continent and vibrations of energies felt on the soles of their feet as Mokèlé-mbèmbé moved to its destination from the mighty forest of the Congo. He was the one send out to destroy the headquarters of Memnon in Namibia. The river tides rose and the Inkanyamba positioned himself in the waters in preparation of the attack from the seas to protect the west coast of Alkebulan. On the east coast Gbahali the crocodile lay in wait. By then Ishtar was not concerned about attacking Memnon directly. His grip on the world was decreasing as the human beings divided by thought and greed took matters in their own hands. The presidents couldn't not agree on anything. Likewise, the citizens within each country were divided and out of control. They too had their own ideas of either isolation as a group or total takeover of the world. Everyone wanted to loot the world for its own personal gain. Memnon had only one interest for now and that was to get his hands on the final scripts of the House of Bulan to invade the city of gold, or at least get to its trail. Thus, he was no longer a threat. It was the people that needed to be saved from themselves and by doing so, rescue the world from a full fledge world war.

Tribal gangs riot the cities just like during the days of apartheid and segregation from the foreigner. The people were separated; black against black killings increased and everyone supporting their own. The few existing shopping outlets were marked such that only relations of the same could shop at an establishment belonging to tribe of the owner. The economy fell entirely as production lines in factories and mines closed. All places where people of all races were working together had to close down as they were out of killing grounds of one against the other. Out of fear for their lives, people started hiding. Those with money built tranches and underground rooms for themselves to hide at night. Others fled into the forest to be out of sight. Those gifted in spiritual wisdom also took to the fight as requested by their people and strike others with strange illnesses and sudden deaths. The cities were deserted once again just like it was three years ago with the experiences of the last pandemic. The world over division in skin colour and race took over and everything came to a standstill. Order was no more and love had no hold in such a time. Children of the soil were feeling the pain and distress as each day millions were dying. If not through tribal killings, they succumbed from hunger. It was only the womb that felt the extinction of human race and relieved the birth pains. The women remembered their error of centuries ago, when she became greedy and jealous of the sister when she closed her eyes against seeing the other women's sorrow and pushed for her personal gain and advancement. When she started manipulating her sons into striving for their personal good and not be their brother's keeper. When she started showing only teeth to her sister instead of smiling genuinely and stabbing her in the back. Because of her, those in polygamous marriages raised their children as step children instead of blood siblings from the same lions. Because of her, the sons grew up fighting for unjust causes only for the benefit of one household. Because of her food was no longer shared and the next of kin suffered alone. The union which was instilled by creation now degraded. The daughters of Amma started to realize that they were at fault as they encouraged their husbands to be in competition with his brother and therefore allowing open access to the cunny Memnon to manipulate their weakness. When she saw her offspring, laying on open graves or dead in the streets because no one could bury them. She realized it was time to call her sons to order but it was late, many lost their lives because she was silent for far too long. She hid her face in the gutter for far too long. Playing into the hands of the cunny master manipulator. Off course, not all was her fault because she didn't know that it was to get out of hand to such a degree. She only acted as being the nurturer of the household while following the broken instructions of those before her. As the House of Bulan was broken down, she had no information to serve the world with wisdom. What she thought was right blew up in her face and caused the world to go under. As the nurturer, unknowingly, she played in the hands of the destroyer because she didn't ask the correct questions. She didn't inquire from where he was coming and what his mission was. She didn't inquire from the priestesses nor followed her own mind. She didn't take care of her house as she needed to. In that hour of recognition of truth, the mother reached out to the only source which could understand her plight and took to the forest. On her knees, she cried out and seek for atonement. Nature was the only source which would understand and forgive her in the presence of the universe. For her atonement with self and nature was important for the clock to change times. If she could convince nature of her repentance, she could petition for another opportunity to serve as a divine womb-men. This time, rising from the gutter a new generation of human beings and not persons divided by colour, sexuality, religion, politics or greed. Given the opportunity, she made an oath to reinvent the times and return to practices more befitting the new generations to be born out of this experience. This mother was not standing single in her quest for all over the world because that night, a light shone on the earth and permission was granted to clean the world. Unfortunately, that didn't mean that those standing in divide were not to be prosecuted. Hence, Ishtar and her army had to roam the cities to make way for the new generation to come.

On the wings of Ninki Nanka, a dragon like creature, Ishtar flew across the continent. The dragon spewed fired on the grasslands to expose it to the sun. For a new order to start, it was important to burn down the old and rebuild a new. Those hiding in the forest were exposed. While many died, some escaped the great fire. These people were taken by the Medicanian light workers and transported to safety at Area 51. Slowly, light workers re-emerge to follow the trail which was light up by night with the rescued people. Each night making sure that the one, ten or hundred found would reach safety. While others were engaged in their duties all across the continent, Mokèlé-mbèmbé reached his destination in Namibia. As if holding a compass to his head, he went straight to the capital city and walked through its streets. His huge physic resembling a dinosaur's weighed tons and stood heavy on the ground. With each step he took the earth trembled. Each step also broke the ground and the trembling made buildings crash to the ground. Memnon was not at his headquarters because he has abandoned it long ago. When he saw how the wheels of the world were turning in his favour, he left everything to go on its course and flee after the light workers went in search of Ishtar. He was observing all their moves and didn't really care to interfere with them. For him to be able to rule the earth, he realized that he needed people thus agreed with the rescue mission that they put in place. He realized that by being clouded with greed he became careless and made very huge mistakes, thinking that total extinction of the human race was going to allow him enough room to play emperor on the piece of soil. But, when the hour of destruction reached, he realized that he couldn't live alone in the entire world. Thus, he gave Ishtar the upper hand to fix what he has destroyed. Once she was done, he figured to step back in and take over. However, for him to do all that he needed the final piece of the puzzle. This he knew was in the hands of Ishtar. Mokèlé-mbèmbé thus reached his destination and destroyed the entire heroes acre from that build within and that which was beneath. Killing the machinery, robots and human species kept beneath the headquarters. His size turning everything to dust. The fall of the heroes' acre signified that the era of commemoration of lost blood came to an end. If the soil was to be rejuvenated, the dead had to bury the dead and the living needed to continue living in the present of time. The whistle thorn acted like a seasoned journalist sending messages left right and center. The fall of the mighty heroes' acre and the headquarters of Memnon was broadcasted through the entire continent. Ishtar and Ninki Nanka celebrated and followed the example to destroy all the statues erected by man in the name of their fallen heroes. Everything that didn't serve the purpose of re-creation was burned down. The spirits summoned by the evil wise men rose with thunder from the seas, both on the west and east coast of the continent and send up storms of water into the mainland. Gbahali and Inkanyamba were ready and stopped them in their tracks. They only allowed enough water into the mainland to quench the thirst of the soil and kill the fire. This started the first exercise to bring back order on the continent. The fire burned out the evil and the water was brought in to cleanse it from dirt and fill it with reason. While nature was restored once again and the unnecessary infrastructures broken down, Popabawa and Tikoloshe journeyed into the hiding places of people to assist the light workers to lead them to safety. Impundulu laid eggs with medicinal powers which the light workers were using to heal the people injured during the war. But to complete the entire exercise, those who are evil had to be uprooted entirely and this is what Adze and Bili Ape did. After months of war, there came a time of silence over the continent. The other continents in the world also lay in ruins with only a few survivors here and there. Complete silence fell over the earth as the human race exhausted all efforts of fighting and lost their energies. They sat in a heap of dust not sure what happened to them and their land. Devastation was felt everywhere and no soul bothered to venture out of its space to investigate the extent of their foolish actions. For days on end, people just sat around, not talking, thinking about the recent days and why they had to carry so much rage within them. Everything was lost. Their hard labour and that which they killed for in the name of greed. In the dark dusty streets there was no luxury. The mothers kept wailing in the open on their knees. Their hearts seeking forgiveness from the source above. Time was returning once again to a new normal and those standing in the knowledge were returning. At that time, Ishtar called out to the Fever, Sausages, Quiver, Leadwood, Marula, Mupane and the Sycamore Fig to return. They had the food and healing that the remaining people of the continent needed to regain their strength. She multiplied them across the continent and people were fed and healed. All warrior animals returned to Area 51. The twelve plants that took an oath to support Ishtar during her mission took over and spread new vegetation in the soil all over the continent. It was a new sight to behold. With the rivers streaming, new waters and the vegetation in pursuit to cover the earth, life was returning and it looked beautiful.

From the other lost continents, people saw the light burning on Alkebulan and returned. This time they were received by the mothers in good faith. Emerged into a new found love people, were waiting upon a new guide for direction. Ishtar knew that the time has come to reveal the truth to the people. The sun went dark and Ishtar lit up the world; revealing her true identity to the people. Many were caught by surprise, mostly those from Namibia who associated her with one of their tribes. She stood majestically in the sky looking at everyone with adoration. Thinking this was indeed a race that would continue in favour of Amma, they would do wrong but also find within themselves the power to raise themselves from extinction. While she stood in the presence of everyone, Memnon also came to the fore. He knew that the hour of revelation has come and that he will be able to find the missing link. Hidden as in the past, a short distance away from the other people, he waited. Ishtar increased her powers and the light became brighter. None of the people could look up as the rays of the light were blinding them. Everyone stood in total silence as transformation was flowing through their bodies. Ishtar's light sent healing energies through their bodies and exposed the mind to see the truth which was hidden from the world for all those centuries. Through Ishtar, the people saw into the chambers of the most holy and divine. They saw the purpose of creation and understood the mission on earth. They saw Amma and understood that he was all; he was in them and also present in the world. They saw a reflection of who they were through his image. Memnon gave an agonizing cry and turned around and fled into the woods. He too had seen what Ishtar revealed to the people. He also saw that he has been chasing after the wrong signs. All those years of fighting and deceiving the people, all those years of seeking that which was right in front of him. He screamed above his lungs and kept running. He needed to distance himself from this world but he knew deep down that there was no escape. Later he stopped in his tracks near a cliff and jumped from it. As he was falling, he received the final script. The one that spoke about love that compasses all understanding. The love that binds the world in perfect peace.

CHAPTER THIRTEEN

Ishtar stands in the presence of Amma, looking down on the people of the earth. It was a deep conquest, where she was allowed to feature into physical and mental bodies which she was not accustomed to. Together with the human race, she trekked through time and space, seeking answers for questions she thought she knew while trying to understand the essence of Amma and why it was important to create the earth and protect it so fiercely. As she bowed before his presence, she knew that he was indeed great and no one could equal him in the universe. His actions were not hidden. They were right in front of them all to see and learn, but objectivity, personal strive and all other little things that they made important kept it hidden from the sight. Such that everybody seek for the truth in the wrong places because the soul hungered after it. He made himself visible from the very beginning but people turned to the other side, for they were conditioned to think that everything in life was to be obtained through hard labour. A readily and free source of joy was just not reasonable and frowned upon with doubt. Alkebulanians were a warrior tribe and victory through sweat was the sweetest experience they hungered for and this didn't justify a reluctant receipt of favour. However, having gone through an extensive trial and error with innocent blood shed and the animal spirit taking over the divine human soul, it was needed for them to taste pain in its greatest form, to experience defeat and lost not seen in millions of years. So that they could appreciate their privilege and gifts. Only when the privilege shifted hands and landed on the wrong side of the world, did they realize that it was worth fighting for it. The privilege of life and its gifts are not to be taken for granted. It required wisdom to implement and see it multiply and respect for the creator and adherences to the principle code it comes with. True worship thus required that they harmoniously engineered to use their favour for the betterment of the world. Gold trail is thus a projection of the journey of life. One where each person seeks the ultimate purpose of life. Innate from birth is the inquiry to the meaning of life and the purpose of creation. The seeking of understanding and wisdom to perfect existence on earth. Through decades, Amma's sons and daughters reincarnated to earth in trying to provide the answers they seek and give direction. However, the species remained hard headed and after the first waves of the new experience fades away, they dwell back again into the falsehood they lived in. Looking at them as they toil to rebuild the lost planet, Ishtar was certain that they were going to succeed in creating yet another dynasty which would be mightier than the ones before. They can and they have the will power to do so. The question was, will it be the last time. Hearing her thoughts, Amma chuckled and look at her. "Child, this species is entirely different and you have seen the evidence thereof." Time will be the ultimate judge to decide who amongst them all gets closer to the truth. Memnon searched for it from the one world to the other. They rushed through millions of theories and convinced themselves to fight for the ones that justified their consciousness best. They ended up wasting many good years of peaceful living and killing innocent souls. You have given them what was availed to you and they have grasped it for now. It is still not the complete picture as people are still not yet aware of the things of the invisible world. They don't understand how powerful the animal mind is that they jointly share with the other species which inhabits the land. They don't even take care of their spiritual lifestyles and strive to purify it and for this matter only, many things are still to be revealed to them. However, the lesson of knowledge has been learned and I know that their minds are flexible enough to view the different principles available in the universe and derive information from it. This will surely bring them closer to the knowledge of physical manifestations of time and space within which they live. Amma's creations are seven worlds, the sun and the moon, within this lays the Kize-uzi an internal vibration which gives way to creations to be manifested. This is what they have within themselves to set them apart from other species.

Humans are a great and wise source to be reckoned with, Memnon just didn't realize that everything he had and everything that he sought after was equally embedded in every human heart and mind. He misread the signs of meekness in the people as a lack of particles of knowledge. Every individual carrying the source of life was able to think and act according to the information provided upon birth. As life conditions them, they are equally allowed to make choices that befits their purpose and stands in alignment thereof. They were given different blue prints as a species simply because a greater being other than Amma wasn't the idea of creation. Particles of Amma were separated in each of them such that over time they would find the link to unite as one powerful and divine force with extensions in all spheres. However, the unseen eye that lacked direction was equally lost to the great purpose of creation. The assistance of Ishtar brought them closer to the threshold of perceiving mysteries of the DNA or spiral structure of Amma which is also found within them. Striving forward, they will use that intelligence to understand the interconnection of live in the galaxies beyond and the energies which binds them as one. Through comprehension of the information they will be able to change a lot of things. They will rise with new scientific trends and outsmart those in Andromeda and other planets. At least they now have access to Area 51 which will clear up many uncertainties. Amma looked at Ishtar hopefully and smiled. "You know I love this species dearly and I have faith in what they can become." He said finally.

Gold trail is a project which I took up as a new year's resolution upon myself. The year 2020, I was to challenge and surprise myself. Indeed, surprises came in many different forms. I started looking at the world through a different lens while doing research for the book. Born and raised as a Black African Christian child, the taboos of religion, ethnicity and culture came back to haunt me with every new lesson learned. I stood in a place where I questioned the truth, while fearing as an upcoming writer that critics would haunt me night and day. Not from the literary world but, those that raised me and those that grown up with me; criticizing the very being of my new tone of writing and questioning my faith. I feared the ultimate question of who God is and why I should believe what I based my story upon. Thus, while it normally takes me a month to draft a raw manuscript from beginning to end this project lasted for six good months. I only wrote the conclusion a week before the marketing of the book commenced. I walked with this book through the trail to rediscover myself. Fear disappeared and restoration set in. I became a new being as the book grew and know that with the vast information obtained during my research, that mentioned in the book and others that I kept hidden in my heart, I will never be the same person again. I found information so great, knowledge so deep but above all the understanding how to be human. Through the pages of this book, I hope that something resonates in your soul and sets you out to seek that one truth that separates us from the carnal and projects divinity for what is it. I hope that you find enlightenment that saves us all from extinction and allows us to live in perfect peace. I hope that through these few pages, you find a word that can light up that urge to stand with me in a quest to rebuilt our world and spread love. I stand with you and those that came before us, for together,r we are human.

To my grandchildren, I look at life through your gentle eyes and know that this is a reminder that life is good and will remain good.

Thank you

Martha Sibila |Khoëses is an experienced administrative professional, poet, speaker and creative writing coach. She is a single mother of two and a grandmother, born and raised in Windhoek, the capital city of Namibia. She now resides in the beautiful little town of Okahandja, Namibia. She always had a passion for creative writing, and after graduating with a Bachelor of English degree obtained at the Namibian University of Science and Technology, she picked up the pen and self-published a series of books in 2018/9. As a postgraduate student and a strong activist of women empowerment, she has started a movement under the title "Let me Dream" based on one of her books, to transform the lives of others all over the globe.

Let Me
Dream
Martha S. Khoeses

Anthology of verse
Moods Awakened
Martha S. /Khoeses

Relive
the
moments
Martha Sibila
Khoeses

Grey Horse
(/Hai hab)
The mysterious horse
rider
Martha Sibila /Khoeses

Sonskyn
Martha Sibila
Khoeses

HOANDI
AND THE CITY
MARTHA SIBILA /KHOÉSES
HOANDI'S
SCHOOL
TRIP
HOANDI
AND
FRIENDS
MARTHA
SIBILA /KHOÉSES
HOANDI'S
CULTURE
DAY
MARTHA
SIBILA /KHOÉSES